Praise for S

"A must read. Sharp, intelligent, and compelling."

"McDowall has a true talent."

"The definition of a page turner."

"Stands shoulder to shoulder with other authors in this genre."

"Powerful. Insightful. Real and gripping."

"Every piece of the puzzle slots together to create the perfect masterpiece."

"A great example of plot, pace, and characterisation."

Other titles by Stewart McDowall

<u>Detective McQueen series</u>

#1, *The Murder Option*
#2, *The Mind Hack*
#3, *The McQueen Legacy*

The Murder Option

Stewart McDowall

SRL PUBLISHING

SRL Publishing Ltd
London

www.srlpublishing.co.uk

First published worldwide by Darkstroke Books in 2021
This edition published by SRL Publishing in 2025

SRL PUBLISHING
THINKING DIFFERENTLY, DELIVERING CHANGE

Text copyright © Stewart McDowall, 2021

The moral right by the author has been asserted in accordance with the
Copyright, Designs, and Patents Act 1988.

ISBN: 978-1915-073-47-1

1 3 5 7 9 10 8 6 4 2

This book is sold subject to the condition that it shall not, by way of trade or
otherwise, be reproduced or transmitted in any form or by any means,
electronic, mechanical, photocopying or otherwise, without the prior
permission of the publishers.

No part of this book shall be used in any manner for the purpose of training
artificial intelligence (AI) systems or technologies.

SRL Publishing and Pen Nib logo are registered trademarks owned by SRL
Publishing Ltd.

This book is a work of fiction. Names, characters, places, and incidents are
either a product of the author's imagination or are used fictitiously. Any
resemblance to actual people, living or dead, events or locales, is entirely
coincidental.

A CIP catalogue record for this book is available from the British Library

SRL Publishing is a climate positive publisher offsetting more carbon
emissions than it emits.

For Tricia, Holly, and Alex

One

It was a cold morning, and a shimmer of pretty frost was glistening across the whole sloping field in the heatless rays of the February sunshine. It sparkled on every blade of grass and every hair on the back of his head. There would have been a cloud of breath coming from his mouth if he had been breathing.

The blood had congealed around a knife in his back. It had pierced his coat then travelled on its deadly journey through his shirt, eased past his skin, crunched through a rib and then punctured his most vital organ. A dagger through the heart — a classic — not much murder imagination, but effective, none the less.

The insistent whine of the approaching quad bike went unheard by Colin Baxter who was past hearing anything ever again, but it stirred up some of the birds in the nearby hedgerow. From the bottom of the field the farmer had thought he was about to encounter yet another one of the bags of fly-tipped rubble that had become the bane of his life.

The Murder Option

The top hedge was next to a quiet road, and it was too easy for criminals to hoist rubbish over the top. However, now that he was closer, he could see exactly what the bulky outline was, and he stopped the bike. Damn, it was going to mean trouble. All kinds of police and officials would come charging over his land now. Police vans would churn up his field. It would probably be cordoned off, too, for how long, and then what? Would ghoulish tourists traipse over everything? Reporters? He sighed. What a pain. There was something he could do, though. It wasn't pretty, but the guy was dead anyway, so what did it matter?

Two

'The police gave up,' said Mrs Baxter, the sombre, respectful widow's tones of her clothing doing nothing to dampen her appealing glow. He knew he was going to like her. 'They said they couldn't find any evidence, so they just gave up.' She raised her hands, palms open, and McQueen nodded. Spread before him on his desk were the police reports and newspaper clippings that detailed the violent and tragic death of her husband. 'That's why I want you to investigate,' she continued. 'I want you to find my Colin's murderer.'

They were sitting opposite each other in McQueen's small office, her in the uncomfortable guest seat back to the window, him on his high-backed swivel chair. The office was an expense he could do without, but he needed it to house his filing cabinets and for these client meetings if nothing else. It also gave him an official business address. He could keep the more unsavoury clients he sometimes acquired away from his home. His office was one of four in the building and he had the room they were in now, a toilet and tiny kitchen all on the ground floor. It was located on a road that led into Leeds city centre and there was always a steady stream of a people trudging by. "Good footfall," the agent had said when he'd first come to view it, and he was right, although little of that people-traffic diverted to his door.

The main road was on a slight rise so, as passers-by on their way to the busy shops and trendy cafés lent forward against the hill, it gave them a sloping shape reminiscent of the figures in a Lowry painting. McQueen's window looked out onto the street but he found it distracting so he kept his vertical blinds angled to almost closed most of the time. The shadows of the passing trade were rhythmically crossing the blinds behind Valerie Baxter even now as she sat telling him her story.

'I can pay,' added Mrs Baxter. 'A little was left to me by Colin, and I think the best way I could use it would be to get him some justice. It's what he'd want.'

McQueen studied the woman in front of him, looking for any discordant signs, anything that might mean in her grief she had lost her grip on reality. The overriding word that came to his mind was *driven*. She had come to him with a clear purpose, and it had ignited a passionate intensity in her dark eyes. She was both a defiant and an attractive forty-something woman, her shoulder-length hair a rich chestnut brown with some playful curls that were untamed by hairspray. She had a straight-shouldered confident posture, but her outward softness did not mask the fact that something tougher lay beneath. McQueen noticed she was wearing almost no make-up, no lipstick, but some colour had been applied to her cheeks, perhaps to disguise the pallor of grief. *Some people are just born good-looking,* he thought, *and there isn't much that detracted from that other than a long-term crack habit or bad plastic surgery.* She had to be at least ten or fifteen years younger than her deceased husband, whose age at the time of death, he'd already seen in the clippings, was fifty-seven. He considered the age difference might have been interesting to find out more about, but it wasn't time for that right now.

McQueen knew some of the tabloids would have their readers believe murders happened all the time, but in this country, for middle-aged men who weren't involved in drug smuggling or some other form of organised crime, they were actually very rare. Like most things which are statistically improbable, when the rare thing happens to you or a loved one, statistics become meaningless. It reminded him the difference between an economic recession and a depression was that a recession was when your neighbour was out of work and a depression was when *you're* out of work. Personal perspective had rendered the rarity of murder an irrelevance to the woman sitting in McQueen's office. Justice had become Mrs Baxter's mission in life, something to live for. She knew it wasn't going to bring her husband back, but what else was she supposed to do, move on? It was one of those popular phrases that sounded great in a self-help book, but was hard to transfer into real life.

'The person who did this needs to be caught and locked up,' she continued, holding McQueen's gaze. 'In fact, if I had my way, they'd be hanged, or better still, boiled alive in oil.' There it was, the first sign that emotion was ruling her thinking. She was very serious, and becoming quite animated, leaning forward like an impassioned Prime Minister at the dispatch box and tapping on the desk. 'But they won't do that these days, will they? A slap on the wrist is all they get and that's it.' Sensing a possible meltdown on its way, he decided to steer her away from the politics of modern verses medieval punishment.

'That's an understandable reaction, Mrs Baxter,' he said, charitably. 'But what makes you think I can do any better than the police? They do have enormous resources at their disposal and, as I understand it, they conducted a very thorough investigation.'

She snorted. 'Thorough? The only suspect they looked at was the farmer, and it turned out all he did was move Colin's body off his land. That's why he had the blood in his trailer. They were convinced it was him, so they spent too long trying to prove it. Meanwhile the real murderer must have been laughing.'

McQueen sat back in his chair to assess how this case was panning out. He'd agreed to meet her because, to be honest, he met anyone who bothered to ring up and make an appointment. You never could tell what was going to unfold even from the most straightforward meetings, but this one was living up to his relatively low expectations. It was a stone-cold no-hoper, a dead-end police investigation where the juices of possibility had been well and truly sucked out of it. Frankly, it was a waste of time. A more cynical private investigator would take her money, make all the right noises, chase up some non-existent leads, build some hopes, and then regretfully dash them. But McQueen wasn't in the business of ripping-off grieving widows. Business wasn't great, but it wasn't *that* bad yet. Still, Valerie Baxter needed some kind of positive noises to lift her day, and he didn't want to send her off into the unscrupulous arms of his competition who would be more than ready to shake her money tree.

'Okay,' he said. 'I'll tell you what I'll do, Mrs Baxter. I'll keep all these documents with me if that's okay and I'll read through them properly? Then, if there's something I think might be fruitful, I'll take the case on, but if I think there's nothing to be gained other than more pain for you and a hole in your bank account I'll tell you and you can save your money. Is that fair?'

She nodded. 'Okay, but all you need to do is go and speak to Harper.'

He'd been wrapping up and was about to shuffle her on out of the office and this threw him a little.

'Who's Harper?'

She pointed at the papers on the desk.

'Martin Harper,' she said as if he should already know. 'Colin's boss. He's the man who killed him. I told the police that right at the beginning, but they did nothing. They were too focused on that stupid farmer and by the time they spoke to Harper he'd had time to cover his tracks.'

It wasn't unusual for a grief-stricken relative to have a suspect in mind. Quite often it was someone they hated already, but he was sure the police would have eliminated from the inquiry an obvious suspect like the boss.

'Why do you think it was this guy Harper?'

She pointed to one of the stapled sheets on the desk. 'It's all in my statement to the police, Mr McQueen. All you need to do is speak to him and you'll see.'

Her point made, she stood up scraping the chair back with the backs of her knees and smoothed down the creases in her black skirt. She was very trim and fit-looking. McQueen found himself wondering if she was one of those running obsessives that seemed to be everywhere these days. As she was preparing to leave, as an afterthought, McQueen did his business market research.

'So, just for my records, Mrs Baxter, can I ask what made you choose to bring this case to me?' he asked. It was a question he didn't much like, but he'd been told by a business advisor it would give him a valuable insight into how to attract more clients. More clients was the item at the top of his list of goals the advisor had made him write down.

'Research,' she answered. 'I looked at a number of private investigators' websites, and yours showed you were the only one that wasn't an ex-policeman. It said you were an academic criminologist.'

'Okay. And you liked the sound of that?'

'To be honest, I don't really know what it means, but I don't trust the police, and an ex-policeman is only going to give me the same lies that the real ones did.'

Unsurprised, McQueen nodded. It was an argument he'd heard before and was the reason he mentioned it on the website.

After she'd gone, McQueen bundled up the papers to take home. Challenging murder cases were few and far between, but were exactly why he'd got into this business in the first place. Missing persons, divorce proceedings, and general lack of spousal trust made up the bulk of his routine work, so he should have been more excited about a case that offered a chance to get back to his field of expertise. But at the moment, all he could smell was frustration and disappointment. An unsolved murder had potential for glory, but also carried with it the weight of lack of police cooperation, even obstruction. They wouldn't want to see an outsider get a result they themselves had failed at. It would be an embarrassment.

Mrs Baxter had seen the fact that McQueen wasn't an ex-cop as an advantage, but in truth, in his line of work, it was much more of a hindrance. The police tended to look after their own. He couldn't rely on cosy chats and information leaked by old pals over a pint in the pub for his leads. There were no favours from old mates he could rely on. No, he had to do it all himself, often pushing against a wall of official silence he had to eke out his own information and pick up his own leads. Usually, that was the part of the job which ignited his interest, the man-alone challenge of it, but at other times the strain of it could turn a simple investigation into a frustrating odyssey of dead-ends and slamming doors. *Still, you never know with a murder*, he thought. *There was always potential for glory*. Besides, he liked Valerie Baxter, and he wanted to help her. He had to wonder if there was anyone who would be prepared to fight for his justice once he was dead. There was certainly no one who would have the dedication that she had.

Three

Since his divorce, McQueen had lived alone in a small, unremarkable two-bedroom flat within walking distance of his office. It suited him fine. It was easy to keep clean, the neighbours were quiet, and he didn't have to bother dragging a lawnmower round a garden every week. When he'd lived in the suburban semi-detached with his wife, Julie, the dreaded but unavoidable downbeat of his life during the summer months had been the weekly lawn duty. It was usually done on a Sunday while he was battling a Saturday hangover.

There were other advantages to his single life. He had the freedom to eat, drink, and do exactly what he wanted, and when he wanted. And it far outweighed any sneaking feelings he had of isolation. His work times were erratic, and he no longer had to apologise for the phone ringing in the early hours, or for not being back to eat when he'd said he would be. He no longer had to suffer the judgmental looks and comments as he opened another bottle of wine, either.

He was sure his ex-wife was enjoying her new life just as much as he was. She had her own successful career, which McQueen sometimes saw on LinkedIn, and she'd recently been promoted to Marketing Director of a large online retailer. She'd never been a stranger to a few late work nights herself, but that had never bothered him. In fact, he'd seen them as small freedoms. He knew he'd been a pain to live with and he didn't blame her for calling it quits. In his mind he rationalised it as the best thing for her, although he knew she'd suffered at the time. In his job he'd seen a lot of marriages break down due to infidelity, and at least there hadn't been any of that mess to clean up. They'd both been too tired from fighting to be bothered with the added complications of anyone else. Unblessed by kids, they now had a good relationship built on the firm foundations of never speaking to one another.

McQueen slouched on the sofa with his evening meal, a large glass of red wine, and a king-sized bag of salt and vinegar crisps. He could imagine the look of distain it would have elicited from Julie. He raised his glass in a silent 'up yours' salute.

McQueen had been told he was very tall when he was at school, but somewhere along the line, while he hadn't been paying attention, height assessment standards had changed. Nutrition was better these days perhaps, and tall kids had become even taller. Now you didn't seem to be considered tall unless you were at least six-four, so at six feet exactly, McQueen never felt as awkwardly lanky as he had in his youth. He had done his upward growing early and then just

The Murder Option

stopped. And with the weight he'd slowly accumulated over the years, he was better proportioned than his teenaged self. Recently, however, he'd had to take a few half-hearted steps towards making sure the gains didn't get out of hand. The steps hadn't got him all the way to the gym, though, and he wasn't doing well on the pizza and drink, either.

In one of those unexplained genetic quirks, just like his father, McQueen's hair had gone grey while he was still in his twenties. It hadn't bothered him that much, and kind women had often said it suited him. It hadn't shown any signs of falling out, at least. In some ways, the premature greying had kept him young in the eyes of his friends, because year after year his hair looked the way it always had. From time to time since his break-up he had brought some very attractive women back to his home, lovely people who invariably shuddered at the sight of his man-cave, depending on how much they'd had to drink. Although the sex was always welcome, the couplings rarely lasted longer than mere one-night stands. In the early post-divorce days, well-meaning friends, seemingly unhappier about his single status than he was, had been keen to set him up with someone new. It was over dinner with one of these perfectly acceptable semi-girlfriends that McQueen had hit on a revelation. She, too, was a psychologist, but had taken the more worthy career path to clinical psychology. They had been talking about the bas emotions of jealousy, suspicion, disappointment, and anxiety that often surfaced in partnerships, and McQueen suddenly realised he had never been more miserable than when he'd been in any in- depth relationship. Clearly he was cut-out to be single, and he tactlessly voiced this to his companion only to see her face freeze into a mixed look of sympathy and horror. There was no sex that night.

With relationships it was all about compatibility, and for now, the single life was turning out to be the one that was most compatible with McQueen's emotional and practical needs.

Hoping to be able to quickly dismiss the Baxter case and get on with the mountain of paperwork left over from other cases, he started to read through the reports she'd left.

The case had suffered a bad start and had never recovered. All physical crime scene evidence had been destroyed by the hapless farmer. The police had easily traced the dumped body back to him because he'd been seen in the woods with his trailer and reported by a birdwatcher who'd even helpfully taken a picture of him in full digital clarity. Initially, the police had jumped to the conclusion that he was their man, and they had thrown their full investigative weight behind proving it. Eventually, however, when no possible connection emerged between the two men, strangers who had never met, let alone a motive for murder emerge, it all began to unravel. Then, crucially, the official time of death of between nine and ten in the morning on Wednesday 11th placed the suspect out of town, and their investigation eventually fell apart. The fledgling case collapsed, the only verdict being the farmer had been a selfish idiot. He'd eventually been charged with obstruction and failing to report a crime, but he wasn't the murderer. By then, any useful forensic evidence from the actual crime scene had been contaminated and was useless.

On examination of the diagrams, descriptions, and photographs, McQueen's first thoughts were that it was a showy murder. A knife, which had turned out to be a standard supermarket carving knife available almost everywhere, was left in his back, and the body had been dumped in plain sight, not buried, hidden, or chopped up. The killer blow had taken some strength and probably wasn't from a woman. Although not impossible, it was unlikely. The stab wound showed some precision. Even though it was dumped over a hedge in a field, the body was bound to be discovered at some point. It was almost a statement, a message, perhaps. McQueen browsed the documents and wrote down the timeline, making notes along the way.

According to Mrs Baxter, Colin had set off to walk to the station as usual to go to work on the Wednesday morning and she had kissed him goodbye. She said he hadn't seemed any different than normal, not worried or distracted in any way. Valerie worked from home at her computer, so she was in all day. Colin never arrived at work, so after a couple of hours someone from the firm had first tried to call his mobile phone, and then when they had no luck they had rung the house to see if he was coming in. The business owner, Mr Martin Harper, was away on business that day and they had expected Colin Baxter to cover for him. That's when Mrs Baxter had started to worry, and by evening when he didn't come home, she tried to report him missing. The police told her that a grown man not coming home for one night didn't count as missing and told her to ring back after another day.

The next day she still hadn't heard anything and

frantically she called the police again explaining how out of character it was for her calm, steady husband to not come home. It had never happened before, she said, and her panic broke through the official indifference so the police told her they would look into it.

On Thursday morning the farmer returned from an agricultural show he'd been at the previous day and went to check on his fields. That's when he'd spotted the dead body of Colin Baxter and tried to move it off his land. By Friday morning he was in custody.

McQueen pushed aside the report, refilled his glass, and picked up Mrs Baxter's statement. He'd expected to read an emotional outpouring of disjointed accusations and gibberish, maybe even some detailed descriptions of culprit torture but as he read on it was with a growing sense of unease and a feeling this wasn't something he was going to easily ignore. By the second page he had resigned himself to the idea that she was right. He needed to speak to Martin Harper. He put the statement aside and went back to the accumulated information Mrs Baxter had managed to get from the police. It was 2am when he finally lifted his feet onto the sofa and closed his eyes.

Four

Waking in your clothes with a pounding headache and an aching neck is never the best start to any day, but it wasn't an unusual feeling for McQueen, and at least some things can be helped, if not fixed, by a hot shower.

There was absolutely no reason Martin Harper should have agreed to talk to him, and McQueen knew he had to handle the call delicately. Harper was the owner and Managing Director of a busy engineering firm, and the deceased had been his right-hand man for twelve and a half years, right up until he had decided to leave to join a rival company. According to Mrs Baxter's statement, something had gone on between them, and her husband had been reluctant to talk about it. She felt Harper was a ruthless and calculating businessman. 'Bastard' was the word she actually used in the statement, who didn't want his secrets going to a competitor and that's why he'd killed Colin. It wasn't much, but people had been killed for less, and it did depend on what kind of secrets Colin had been keeping.

What was more intriguing to McQueen was why the police had failed to follow up on Harper. The grieving wife was right, they didn't seem to have done very much to chase him up, and he hadn't even been questioned as far as McQueen could see. He dug down the side of the sofa on which he'd fallen asleep and retrieved his phone. He blinked his blurry eyes and sent a text to Mrs Baxter saying that after reading her documents he had decided to take on the case and start with a week of his time before reviewing. He told her how much it would cost and to let him know if she still wanted him to continue.

The answer came back within minutes. The costs were fine, but had he a chance to speak to Harper yet? He shook his head and threw the phone back onto the couch. He'd never been a big fan of micro-management. If he was going to pursue any case it was at his own pace and in his own order and, right now, a shower and coffee were his priorities. He needed to look and feel slick if he was going to face Martin Harper. He might only get the one chance, so had to make the best of it. Someone like Harper was unlikely to be impressed by a half-shaven, red-eyed man in a creased shirt who still smelled of the day before. *Pride,* he thought. *Show some pride.*

Ever since McQueen moved to Leeds with Julie all those years ago to pursue his career after completing his doctorate at UCL in London, he found the people there to be achingly proud. They were proud of their city, proud of their football team, and insanely proud of being proud. It was an added layer on top of the underlying birth-right pride in being from Yorkshire. It was odd, though, they often made a loud virtue

The Murder Option

of being mean with money, when in fact McQueen had experienced warmth, kindness, and generosity that far outstripped the anonymous coldness of London. However, being a southerner had not always helped McQueen to be accepted. He knew he would have to tread carefully with Martin Harper or risk a blunt and final rebuff.

Five

'So you're looking into Colin Baxter's estate?' asked Harper, checking out the business card McQueen had handed him and smiling pleasantly.

'Yes, that's right. Just tying up some loose financial ends, finding people who might be owed money, that kind of thing. It's all just paperwork for probate.'

Harper had agreed to meet after McQueen had vaguely dangled the carrot of a possible pay-out of some kind but, even so, he'd only granted him ten minutes from his busy calendar. It had been arranged by Harper's P.A. who, oblivious to the sad cliché of the phrase she'd used, had actually said it was *more than her job was worth* to give him more time than that.

'Well, I can't imagine there's anything in the will for me,' grinned Harper.

'Okay, but did you have any personal loans? Anything that might not show up on any official records?' The older man thought about it for a second, perhaps wondering if it was worth making something up, but in the end shook his head.

'No, I think me and Colin were all square. All debts paid, you could say.'

McQueen had expected to find a well-fed heavy man basking in the success of his company, but Harper was trim and sleek and looked at least ten years younger than his sixty years. He was every inch the charming salesman, salesmanship being the key component of every successful businessman McQueen had ever met. He looked like the kind of guy who kept himself in shape with exercise and healthy living, and he exuded energy. There was probably a lesson for McQueen, whose head had only just stopped throbbing.

'You were good friends, though, weren't you, for many years?'

'Yes, I suppose we were. But I like to keep my business and social life separate. We didn't spend any time together out of the office. There were no golf bets to pay off or anything, if that's what you're thinking.' He checked his watch and McQueen could sense his window of access was rapidly closing. Harper could already see there was nothing in this for him, and he wasn't about to waste any more time. McQueen had no choice but to try to shake him up.

'It was an odd thing, though, wasn't it, Colin's murder? I mean, they never caught anyone. Who do you think did it? Were you ever questioned by the police?' He had tried to make it sound like no more than idle curiosity, but the business shark was not fooled.

Harper narrowed his eyes, sat a little straighter in his chair, and pursed his lips.

'Right,' he said, tapping the business card. 'Now I get it. Private investigator. Makes sense now. Who do you work for, dear old Valerie?'

'I can't disclose who my clients are, Mr Harper, but I can assure you I'm just filling in some missing paperwork.'

'Course you are,' said Harper quite nastily. 'And it's time to take your paperwork, shove it up your backside, and head out of the door. I know she thinks I had something to do with Colin's death, but the police don't, and that's all that matters.' Busted. There was no point continuing the charade. McQueen had been rumbled, he went for broke so he could at least see the reaction.

'He was leaving, though, wasn't he, going to a competitor? That couldn't have been comfortable for you.' Harper was standing now and there was no trace of the charming host left in his face.

'Out,' he barked, pointing at the door. 'Out before I get a couple of lads from the warehouse to throw you out.'

McQueen shrugged and unhurriedly stood.

'Fair enough, Mr Harper. Interesting response to an innocent question, but thanks for your time.'

'If you have any more questions pass them on to my solicitor, because he's the one you're going to be dealing with if you continue to harass me.'

McQueen turned and opened the door, and then Harper spoke in his loud and commanding M.D voice. 'And for your information, he wasn't leaving, I'd given him a raise and he'd changed his mind. I bet Valerie didn't tell you that, did she? If you want to hassle anyone, you should be talking to her weird brother. That's all I'm going to say, now piss off.'

The Murder Option

As McQueen was leaving, Harper's P.A. looked away nervously not wanting to catch his eye and started fussing with some papers on her desk. McQueen assumed she was embarrassed by her boss's rude goodbye, she couldn't have helped but hear it through the open door.

'Don't worry,' he said breezily. 'I can find my own way out,' although she'd shown no signs of getting up to show him out.

Six

In the safe confines of his office, McQueen listened again and mulled over the digital recording he'd surreptitiously made of the morning's brief meeting. He carried a voice activated recorder at all times, mainly to make up for his unreliable memory. The discussion was short and anything but sweet, although unusable as evidence, the recording was useful to add some flesh to his notes. It also helped cement Martin Harper in his mind as a very credible suspect. McQueen recognised Harper as a type. He was the kind of boss who would use a private investigator himself.

Setting up the agency had not been easy, and he'd quickly come to realise his romantic vision of private detective work was just that, a fantasy. Where there was misery and distrust, there were opportunities for private investigators. As well as the tedious and distasteful spousal surveillance work that came his way, there were a whole host of equally dull corporate investigations McQueen had been asked to do. There were the cases of company theft where bosses believed that stock or money was going missing. Sometimes he'd had to interview staff and pore through hours of CCTV footage. A thief's greatest fear was being the victim of a thief. When you have a chiselling money grabbing mind-set you naturally assume everyone is like you. There were the messy cases of unauthorised absence, which dove-tailed nicely into the surveillance of staff who might have been falsely claiming sick pay.

Companies often lived in fear of the guy who was signed off for a bad leg but still played five-a-side every night. Once or twice McQueen had been asked to act as a fake client to gauge what was being said to new prospects, and he'd once caught a guy steering new customers to his own personal, cheaper service. Sometimes he'd had to follow fraud through the labyrinth, although accountants were better placed than him to do that kind of work.

All these jobs generally came from bosses like Harper, and it had left McQueen with a slight dislike of people like him. The guy had the nasty air of a bully about him, so McQueen found himself hoping that he did turn out to be guilty. At the same time, he knew it was dangerous to think like that. The self-made minor tycoon might have a shitty personality, but it didn't make him a killer, and McQueen couldn't afford for his judgement to be influenced by dislike. For all its brevity, the meeting hadn't been a total disaster because the anger and over-reaction to a few basic questions told their own story. He was certainly acting like a man with something to hide. Also, Harper's final attempt to point the finger somewhere else with the mention of the brother was telling. It was something else to check. Maybe Valerie Baxter's brother would have something to say about Harper, too.

What McQueen really needed was some police insight. Why hadn't they questioned Harper at the time? McQueen didn't have a direct line to the police, but he had the next best thing, and it was time to use it. He was about to make a call when the phone in his hand rang from a withheld number.

'Hello? Mr McQueen?' It was a tentative woman's voice.

'Yes. How can I help?'

'Hello. I work at Harper Engineering and I saw you come in today. I got your number from the card you left with Mr Harper.'

'And you are?'

'I don't want to give my name.'

'Okay, you don't have to if that makes you feel more comfortable, but do you have something you want to tell me?'

In the past, McQueen had got a lot of mileage from anonymous tip-offs, although their usefulness when it came to court cases was limited as they were easily dismissed as rumour and hearsay. Their usefulness was more that they could lead you to look in the right places.

'Yes, but you must understand, I don't want to get into trouble,' continued the nervous voice. McQueen knew he had to tread carefully, to coax rather than quiz, otherwise he risked scaring off his only lead so far. Whoever it was had gone to the trouble of getting his number and making the call. It probably wouldn't be that hard to work out who it was. He'd have put money on it being the P.A., but at that moment

The Murder Option

it didn't matter.

'No one needs to know,' assured McQueen. 'So, what do you want to tell me?'

'It's probably nothing, just something silly really.'

'Okay. It doesn't matter if it's silly. You can get it off your chest and then forget about it.' On the other end he heard her take a deep breath as she prepared herself.

'Well,' she said at last. 'I heard Mr Harper and Mr Baxter having an argument a week before he was killed. I liked Colin. He was a very nice man. He was always very kind to me, and I'd never heard him shout before that's why it struck with me. I wasn't earwigging. The door was closed but I could still hear them.'

'I understand. You weren't trying to listen, but did you hear what they were arguing about?'

'Well, that's it. What I remember is that Mr Harper said, "you're always doing this, Colin, you go behind my back and take these decisions yourself, you're a back-stabber Colin."'

'Was that about him wanting to leave?'

'I don't know about that, but then Colin shouted, "no, you stabbed me in the back over Valerie."'

'Valerie? Mrs Baxter?'

'It must have been. She's the only Valerie I know of.'

'Did you hear anything else?'

'No. I knew I shouldn't be listening, so I left. What struck me was that it was how Colin died, wasn't it? He was stabbed in the back.'

'Did you tell the police?'

'I was waiting for someone to ask me if I knew anything, but no one ever did, and then time went by and I couldn't bring myself to call the police because I knew I'd have to make an official statement, and I don't want to do that.' She had unloaded her burden and now just wanted to end the call. 'I have to go now,' she said. 'I've already said too much. I just wanted someone to know.'

McQueen had started to ask if the mystery voice thought that Harper could have killed Baxter, but the line was already dead.

Seven

Anne Kirkpatrick was a very good local journalist, but whether she was actually a good person was open to debate. She had the questionable morality of a hardened journalist and in the past McQueen had used that to his advantage. He'd been able to give her helpful snatches of information which led to some very good stories for her, but only when it suited him. Sometimes the best way to put pressure on people was to have the press shine a spotlight on their lives. A little unflinching press interest always shook people up a bit when they thought they'd got away with something.

Reading through the various clippings Valerie had left for him, McQueen had spotted that Anne had been the one covering the Baxter story, so he now wanted to find out if there was anything more she knew. Anything that had never made it to press. Journalists were a goldmine of gossip and rumour but, even in the wild-west terrain of the internet, for real papers editors existed to make sure only the legally-supportable got published under their name.

A business lunch in McQueen's glamourous world was usually a sandwich and a cup of coffee in the car, but for Anne Kirkpatrick, part of the deal was always that it had to be a pub lunch which was a perfect arrangement for McQueen. As far as he could tell she wasn't exactly an alcoholic, she was no worse than him, but alcohol certainly helped any conversation they'd ever had. Someone had once told him that good journalists existed on cigarettes and coffee, but Anne had different fuel requirements. Even so, she was never anything other than razor sharp, and McQueen always had to be aware he couldn't say anything that wouldn't be remembered and filed away somewhere. He knew someday his own story may need to be exposed and he was sure should that day ever come, Anne would be ready and waiting to drive any necessary nails into his coffin.

Another discrepancy and contrast with the accepted view of crusading journalists that Anne presented was she was always immaculately and expensively dressed, with perfectly arranged hair and make-up to match. Some of the shimmering colour schemes on her eyelids belonged in art galleries. He'd asked her about that once, as to why most of her colleagues favoured the just-got-out-of-bed look and she'd said that if she was blending in anywhere, she would rather it be with royalty than plebs because money and power was where the good stories were.

For his part, as was the case today, McQueen wore a suit and an open necked shirt for most meetings. It was the generally expected work-place uniform if you wanted clients to take you seriously, especially if you were visiting a

The Murder Option

business owner. They liked to see respect being shown. However, he revised his dress code depending on the job. New technology companies and advertising agencies tended to be a bit more casual, and if you turned up in a suit, they were likely to dismiss you as no more than an estate agent. The other reason for McQueen to sling on some jeans for work was when he was going to be sitting in his car all night or crawling through a muddy garden to take some photographs. He couldn't afford to ruin a good suit on every surveillance operation.

For Anne, he wore his best dark suit, it was called "mirroring" in psychological therapy parlance. Creating a bond by reflecting back at the subject the values they hold dear.

Anne's Caesar salad and his scampi and chips had arrived, and they both had a glass of wine in hand before Anne said, 'Okay, you said you wanted to ask about the Baxter case?'

'Yes, do you remember it?'

She rolled her eyes. 'How could I forget an unsolved murder on our patch? Why do you want to know?'

'I've been asked to take another look at it.'

'Who by? The wife?'

'I can't say,' he smiled. 'Like you can't reveal your sources.'

'Okay, well as she's the one who's approached the paper on a regular basis, trying to get us to go over all the old ground, she would be my guess. Anyway, it doesn't matter. If anything comes out of this, I want to be the first to know, okay?'

'Of course. You always are. Now, in the beginning your paper went pretty hard after the farmer.'

'Peter Bainbridge? Yes. We were being fed information by the police, and he was a good suspect. Aggressive, ugly, surly, blood in his trailer. Made a good story.'

'But it wasn't him.'

'No, and that was a story, too. *Police bungle investigation. Wrong man accused.*'

McQueen knew her well enough to know he could afford a little anti-journalist dig at this point.

'That's the key difference between you and me, Anne, I'm after the truth and you're after the story.'

She shrugged. 'Good stories make click-bait, click-bait makes good advertising revenue, good revenue pays my wages. And be honest, McQueen, you wouldn't be the slightest bit interested in the truth if you weren't being paid to find it.'

'Okay, true, true, but tell me, why didn't the police question Martin Harper? He seems like an obvious suspect.'

'The big boss? Oh, they did speak to him, but it was all off the record.'

'Really? Why?'

Anne looked at her empty glass and McQueen taking the hint signalled the waiter. When he'd returned and refilled both their glasses she said, 'My opinion?'

'Whatever you have.'

'Well they didn't want to make another cock-up like the farmer, but there is something else. They'll deny it had any bearing but Harper has some sort of dodgy connection who is said to be a very senior figure in the police force. Their official line is that no one other than the detectives had anything to do with the case, but that's bullshit. A high-profile local murder case? The top brass will have been all over it like flies. Their influence will have been felt all the way down the line. You know what the police are like. They close ranks. Offend the wrong boss and your career is down the toilet. We heard all kinds of things, but nothing that could be used. We couldn't mention anything at the time otherwise they'd have been down on us like a ton of bricks.' For a journalist, Anne used a lot of clichés but then so did her column in more ways than one. Everyone was in a journalistic, short-hand pigeon-hole to Anne, her judgement was instant and usually damning.

They chatted some more about the case, and McQueen asked about Valerie's brother, the one Harper had tried to point the finger at, but Anne had no information on him. As they were winding up their session Anne said, 'You're surprising me, you haven't asked me about the juicy bit.'

'Which is?'

'The other reason the police were inclined to ignore Mrs Baxter's bitter accusations.'

'Which was?'

She was enjoying something about the thing she was about to say, and that's why she was stringing it out.

'The fact that it's strongly rumoured that your truth-seeking Valerie Baxter had a fling with Martin Harper not long before the murder and, as he was the one who broke it off, she carries a bit of a grudge.' McQueen couldn't hide his surprise.

'Valerie Baxter? Really?' He shouldn't have been

shocked, if there was one thing the job had taught him it was not to judge any book by its cover. She may have presented the image of a grief-stricken dedicated widow, but it might have made sense that part of her mission to convict Harper was based on a relationship gone bad. She was a good-looking woman and he was a narcissistic ego behind a desk, so it wasn't a great leap. Still, McQueen found himself slightly disappointed in her taste in men.

'Only a nasty rumour, of course. Not enough to print. But I'd put my house on it.'

They'd finished their meals and the eager waiter bustled over with the bill. McQueen could see a hopeful couple at the door waiting for their table. It was the kind of thing that usually annoyed him and made him take his time, being rushed out to make room for the next punters, but he wanted to get back to the office anyway, and Anne didn't seem to have anything else to tell him. As they were leaving, McQueen turned to her.

'Okay, come on,' he said. 'If you had to make an educated guess, who would you say killed Baxter?'

She thought for only a second. 'I suppose I'd have to go with Harper, but there's absolutely no way of proving it, and if it turned out to be a random stranger killing it wouldn't surprise me either. I don't think we'll ever know.'

Eight

Back at his office, McQueen intended to finally take care of some of the paperwork still outstanding from previous cases, but as soon as he opened his computer, his spirits fell, and he could tell he was too distracted to fight his way through it. The lunchtime wine was having a dulling effect on his passion for routine admin. The Hollywood film image of a P.I. who wore a trench coat and kept a bottle of whisky in his bottom drawer didn't fit McQueen. He didn't like whisky, he only drank wine, which was one of the reasons he didn't consider himself a problem drinker. He could usually stay sober all day and binge a bit in the evenings, but lunchtime socialising was always something of a bump in the road.

Not for the first time, he thought about his life choices and how many of them had been mistakes. He'd had a very stable position as a lecturer in criminology when he and Julie were in the latter stages of their marriage and, although it wasn't exactly lucrative, along with her rapidly growing salary as she moved up the corporate ladder, it gave them a steady, comfortable life. He had swapped all that for the uncertainty, instability, and romance of being a private investigator. What had he been thinking? Stupidly, he'd been imagining he might actually be able to help people and contribute something real to society. His glorious vision had been to put into practice the theories and ideals he'd championed in the lecture hall, but the real life and real people it contained had thrown some spanners into his idealistic works.

It made him think of his father who had never understood why he had wanted to study psychology in the first place. A fiercely proud working-class Glaswegian of the old school, he'd thought that "head-doctoring", as he called it, pronouncing it *heed*, was all nonsense. To him it was all clap-trap made up by university layabouts and reflected nothing of the world he knew. In his father's day, men just got on with it no matter how hard life was, and for him that had been pretty hard. His vision of doing something useful was forging something out of steel that could be touched with your hands, bought and sold, and would last forever. Thinking of heed reminded McQueen of the only advice he'd ever received from his father: "Dinnae ferget the heed, son," he would say, tapping his forehead. From some fathers that would have been an entreaty to always think first but from his father it was the reminder that in a fight the power of the head-butt shouldn't be overlooked. The Glasgow Kiss had become something of a cliché, but McQueen's father had been an early advocate and proponent.

McQueen had never felt he'd quite lived up to his father's expectations. He wasn't tough enough, good enough

The Murder Option

at football, or a big enough drinker. As a boy, he hadn't even liked dripping on toast, the congealed excess fat from the meat pan, spread thickly on hot toast with a hefty sprinkling of salt, or "death on toast" for a man with a bad heart, as he'd once heard it called, a prophesy that came true when McQueen's father had dropped dead at fifty-one after an arduous nightshift at the factory.

His father's distain aside, as a psychology academic, McQueen had run a very popular course. It seemed everyone wanted to hear about serial killers and what made them tick. McQueen's presentations were always fully attended. One topic that had always gone down particularly well he'd called, The Murder Option. As he was sitting in front of his screen, he found himself dipping into his past. In a few clicks he discovered the lecture files, opened his old lecture notes, and began to scan through. He could remember the rapt attention and silence in the room as he began:

A well-educated American man is married to a beautiful and loving wife. They have two lovely daughters who dote on their dad. But Dad meets a new, young woman at work and falls in love with her. Sad, but hey, it happens. Quite often. So, Dad is facing the prospect of breaking the distressing news to his wife and kids that he is leaving to start a new life with his new love. He'll have a painful divorce, and he'll have to pay alimony and child support. It's painful and expensive, but that's what 99.99 percent of men in this position end up doing. The violence and fighting happens, verbally in court, through lawyers, and that's as brutal as it gets.

But then there's the tiny minority.

These are the rare few who want a clean break and a fresh start, so they choose the murder option. And this is a true story, ladies and gentlemen. This happened. This guy, for some reason, chose to murder his wife and the kids and dump their bodies hoping to get away with it. Fortunately, he didn't fool the authorities, but what made him callously choose an option that, thankfully, most people don't even contemplate, let alone carry out? That's what we are going to be discussing today.

He stopped reading and closed the file. That's what he needed to find here, the one who took the murder option. Who was it who thought murder was the best way to deal with whatever problem Colin Baxter had given them? A lot of arrows were pointing in Martin Harper's direction and the office argument the anonymous telephone voice had reported made more sense if Anne's rumour of an affair had been true. He reasoned it out. Baxter felt stabbed in the back by his boss and his wife, while Harper perhaps felt stabbed in the back by Baxter threatening to leave? But would he have taken the step of making the figurative phrase a reality? If Baxter had knifed Harper, it would make more sense. An angry, deceived husband taking drastic steps to take bloody revenge would have been much neater, but the perfect poetic symmetry was spoiled by him being the one who'd ended up dead.

McQueen needed to catch up with Valerie Baxter, but first he wanted to speak to her brother. Harper had said he was weird, and McQueen wanted to judge for himself how weird that was. Strange enough to kill? Different people have different judgement scales, and McQueen's was pretty robust.

He didn't want to alert Valerie he was going to see her brother because he wanted to avoid her priming him. He wanted to catch him with his guard down, if possible. It gave him more chance of getting some straight answers if the guy wasn't prepared for him coming.

Nine

It was basic bread and butter stuff for McQueen to track down Valerie's brother with some rudimentary internet research, and he soon discovered his name was Michael Jarvis. He had an interesting background, too. He'd trained as a doctor but not passed the final exams and never qualified. He now seemed to be working for himself in some sort of business consultancy role. McQueen decided to turn up unannounced to see if he would get flustered and talkative.

McQueen pressed the bell and waited, taking in the pristinely neat garden until, eventually, Jarvis answered the door of the prim Victorian house that served as both his home and his business address. A thick-set, muscular man in his early thirties with a good head of dark hair, he had the familial look of his sister, something difficult to define around the eyes and jaw. In fact, he looked faintly familiar to McQueen which must have been something to do with the way he stared with a deep intensity like his sister as he

The Murder Option

weighed up the man at his door. He must have been happy with what he saw because his face broke open into a very pleasant, warm smile he now levelled at his unexpected caller.

'Hello?' he said in a friendly enough tone. 'Can I help you?'

'I hope so, Michael. My name's McQueen, I'm a private investigator and your sister has asked me to look into the death of your brother-in-law. Can I come in?' Michael Jarvis was anything but flustered and welcomed McQueen inside. He was shown through to a modern, open-plan kitchen, bathed in the morning light allowed by the huge windows. It was a wide space, big enough for a family to use, but in scanning the room, McQueen saw no signs of other occupants.

They sat at a large pine table and Michael offered coffee, which McQueen accepted. There was never enough in his system to compensate for his regular drinking. A battle was always raging in his blood stream between alcohol and caffeine.

'She didn't tell me she had actually hired someone,' said Michael. 'Although she's been talking about it for ages. She's convinced Martin Harper killed poor Colin and that he's got away with it.'

'Yes, she is. What about you? Are you convinced?'

Jarvis shrugged. 'I don't really know. No one does. I can see why he could have done it, and I can see why she thinks it, but it's a big step to accuse someone of murder.'

'You say you can see why he could have done it. Why do you say that?'

'Well, Colin was going to leave Harper Engineering and

take all his knowledge with him. You must have heard that. Martin Harper had relied on him for years and never paid him what he was worth, so it was a pigeon coming home to roost as they say.'

'And how did you get on with your brother-in-law?'

Jarvis paused and frowned a little. 'Sorry, am I a suspect now?'

'No, no, of course not.' McQueen grinned reassuringly and waved away the suggestion.

'Because my alibi is solid if I need one,' countered Michael. 'I was actually with my distraught sister when we first heard that Colin hadn't turned up for work. It was very upsetting.' It sounded a little defensive to McQueen's ear, but he didn't want to alienate Jarvis and have another Harper situation before he'd had a chance to ask any questions, so he back-peddled.

'I assure you, Michael, I'm just trying to get some background colour. I'm trying to paint a picture of what kind of man he was so I can try to shed some light on what happened.' He seemed suitably calmed by McQueen's non-threatening noises.

'Well, I can tell you Colin and I were on friendly terms. He'd been part of my family for about twenty years, so we got on pretty well. I wouldn't say we were particularly close. We never saw each other outside family gatherings, but my only criteria for judgement was whether he was good for Valerie.'

'And was he?'

'I suppose so. But you'd have to ask her that. You see, Mr McQueen, Valerie and I had some tough times as kids. We

The Murder Option

had a very strict upbringing and we've always looked out for each other. So as long as she was happy, I was happy.'

'And what about Martin Harper? Was he good for Valerie?' Again, Jarvis narrowed his eyes.

'Strange question to ask me. I don't know what you mean. He was Colin's boss, so the fact he employed her husband, I suppose, yes, he was good for her in that respect.'

'You know, it's just that she seems to have a strong dislike for him.'

'I suppose if you truly believe that someone killed your husband, you're bound to hate that person, aren't you?'

McQueen took a moment to make a note in his book but at the same time to try to soak up the essence of the man he was facing. What was it about Michael Jarvis? It was nothing he said or anything about the way he was acting, but there was something off-beat about him McQueen couldn't put his finger on. Was it because he was looking for a flaw after Martin Harper's parting shot?

'I know what your sister thinks, but what do you think about Harper?' asked McQueen bluntly.

Michael sighed heavily. 'I have to declare an interest,' he said. 'Because you'll hear about it sooner or later. On Colin's recommendation a couple of years ago, I went for a job at Harper's company. It was a consultancy job and, what can I say, we just didn't hit it off. He's a very impressive guy, Martin Harper. He's built that empire up himself and has some very clear ideas about how to run his business. His style isn't the same as mine. I have a more modern laid-back approach, you could say, less instinct more analytics. Anyway, bottom line is that I didn't get the job. That's why

I'm reluctant to point any fingers at him. It would be easy for him to say I was bitter.'

'And are you bitter towards him?'

'No, not at all. On a personal level I just found him a little bit strange, a bit weird.'

'You thought he was weird? That's interesting, Michael, because that's how he described you.' McQueen was trying to shake him up, to get a reaction that might loosen his tongue, but he just smiled. He was a pretty calm and controlled character.

'Well, there you are, two people on different wavelengths.'

McQueen took a final slurp from the coffee mug. It was strong, and he could feel it winning the fight to revive his sluggish mind.

'And if Valerie is wrong and it wasn't Harper, then who do you think could have killed Colin?' asked McQueen, aware it was pretty much the same question that had got him thrown out of his last interview.

'I have absolutely no idea,' answered Michael, shaking his head. 'And I don't envy you the job of trying to find out. Colin was a very, very nice man. One of the good guys, as they say.'

McQueen was listening for the jarring chime of insincerity, but heard none. He had more questions. He'd barely got started, but Jarvis stood up.

'You'll have to excuse me now, Mr McQueen. I have an online meeting to attend, and I must get on. I'm not sure I've been any help, I'm afraid, but I really can't tell you much. I'm sure the police can give you more useful information than I

The Murder Option

can.'

'Well, the problem is, I don't always have the best working relationship with the police,' McQueen shamefully admitted. 'So I like to get my own information. But if you're busy, I understand.'

He didn't try to outstay his welcome but knew he could come back again for further questions, so he stood up too, thanked Jarvis for his time and coffee, and made his way to the door. He handed Jarvis a business card.

'As they say in all the best cop dramas, if you think of anything that might help, please ring anytime.'

Jarvis studied the card in his hand and then asked,

'Were you always a private investigator, Mr McQueen?' There it was again, that odd note in his voice.

'No, not always. I was a criminologist and a lecturer before this, watching from the side-lines you might say, until I jumped into the cold, shark-filled water.'

'Fascinating,' said Michael scrutinising the card. 'Ah, I see, hence the Ph.D. You're *Doctor* McQueen, then?'

'Yes, but I don't use the title and as you can see it's not on my card, it's not always useful to distance yourself from the crowd in my line of work. Besides, I hate having to explain to people I'm not a proper doctor. They always want to show me their rashes.' He was grinning, trying to leave upbeat. 'I understand you trained to be a medical doctor yourself, didn't you, Michael?'

'Well,' said Jarvis modestly, 'as you'll have heard, I didn't qualify. In the end I couldn't hack the pressure of the exams.' He opened the door and stood to the side to let McQueen walk outside. 'Strange how lives roll on and careers develop, isn't it?' said Jarvis with another friendly smile and closed the door before McQueen could answer.

He was certainly a bit odd, but McQueen liked him. He was intelligent and friendly, and he didn't seem to be so hung up on blindly pinning the murder on Harper, as his sister had been. It might be possible to find out things from him that Valerie had too much tunnel vision to see.

Ten

McQueen had gone back to his flat rather than the office. He had no appointments scheduled but there was someone he wanted to see later and he wanted to change out of his suit. It was one of those times where he thought a more relaxed and approachable image might be better for the meeting, rather than alienating formal and superior.

He'd pored over the crime scene forensic reports but there was precious little to learn from them. When Bainbridge, the farmer, had moved the body, he had destroyed any chance of gleaning any insights, and then when he became a chief suspect his questioning took a different turn, so anything he'd seen was lost. McQueen felt the guy might have something valuable to add, but he'd never really been asked. He knew it would be a tough conversation. He appeared to be quite a truculent character and, given he'd been prosecuted on the back of his actions, he was likely to be less than cooperative. Nevertheless, McQueen felt it might be worth an attempt at appealing to his better nature. It was an avenue no one had tried yet, and there may have been some gold in it.

As McQueen was preparing to leave, he was surprised by a knock at the door, and he opened it to see two young, uniformed police officers. They introduced themselves and he knew he didn't have to but McQueen invited them in hoping to keep it friendly. He had an uneven relationship with the local police. Sometimes they saw him as only an annoyance, but sometimes as a major distraction and thorn in their sides. Very quickly McQueen picked up that these two weren't looking to make friends. They were taking a very official line. They had come to inform him that Mr Martin Harper had made a formal complaint of harassment against him. His complaint was that McQueen had booked a meeting under false pretences and then badgered him about a murder that had nothing to do with him. His solicitor was in the process of instigating a restraining order banning McQueen from approaching Mr Harper. The police advice was to stay away from Mr Harper and to keep his nose out of an on-going investigation.

Their aim was to intimidate him, but McQueen was not intimidated.

'So, tell me,' he said to the copper doing all the talking. 'If it's an on-going investigation, why was Martin Harper never officially questioned by you lot?' The policeman, his authority challenged, took on a more aggressive forceful stance. McQueen looked past him at the even younger one standing behind him. The dynamic was clear; the slightly older one was showing off for the younger one in a this-is-the-way-we-deal-with-private-investigators way. He was a little red-faced now.

'I cannot discuss the details of a case that is still under investigation, Sir. This case is not closed, and if you poke your nose in and get in the way you may well be charged with obstructing justice. We are the professionals and you are an amateur. You lot are just an unlicensed and unregulated pain in the backside as far as I'm concerned, so if I were you, I'd back off. Now.'

He was partially right, thought McQueen. It was true that you didn't need a license to be a private investigator in the U.K., but he took offence at *amateur*. He couldn't think of a harder way to make a living right now.

'Right,' said McQueen calmly. 'Thanks for the tip, officer. And if this unlicensed amateur manages to find the killer that all the power of the professional police force couldn't uncover, you and your investigation might look a bit weak.' *Weak* was a carefully chosen word given the puffed chest he was facing.

'You've been officially warned,' said the police officer, and they started to leave. The youngest one went out first and then the other one turned to lean in and whisper to McQueen. 'If I were you I'd pay attention, Mr McQueen. Remember, very dangerous things can happen out there on those streets when no one is watching. Leave the real criminals to the police and stick to following cheating husbands around.'

McQueen smiled warmly straight back at the bloated face that was within an inch of his own. He wasn't going to be easily baited into saying or doing anything that could give the police any cause to escalate their interest.

'Sound advice. Thank you, officer,' he said, grinning, and shut the door. He watched from the window as the police car pulled away.

'Okay,' he said aloud. 'Now it's getting interesting.'

Eleven

The road was deeply rutted and more suited for a tractor than his car, and he bounced around as he weaved from side to side trying to avoid the deeper potholes. The open gate had a large *No Entry* sign swinging from it, but as it was wide open, he chose to ignore the sign and drove on into the farmyard. On one side of the open yard was a large barn with a corrugated metal roof and a huge sliding door which was closed. On the other side of the yard were some dirty looking out-buildings, from where he could hear the noise of chickens. At the end was an old red-brick farmhouse. Around the yard were various examples of discarded and rusty farm machinery, none of which McQueen recognised. He couldn't even have guessed at their original agricultural uses. As farmyards go, this one had the look of a tired and messy set-up, perhaps indicating that Bainbridge was too busy to bother with aesthetics.

He left the car and first tried the farmhouse, but there was no answer to his knocking. He thought of trying the door, but as his hand reached for the handle he reminded himself that walking uninvited into farm houses was a good way to end up on the wrong end of a double-barrelled shot gun, so instead he walked back to the yard. He shouted for Mr Bainbridge. Although there were various animal noises all around there was no shout back. The farmer could be out in the fields somewhere, he supposed, and he wasn't about to start trekking over the countryside looking for him. He had tried to phone ahead but the number had rung and rung without even the relief of an answer-phone message.

As he was preparing to get back in his car, McQueen looked at the large barn to his left, and the hairs on his neck bristled. He wasn't sure if he had heard anything but felt as if he was being watched, so he wandered over to it. Shouting first that he was coming in, he slid open the huge metal door noisily and peered inside. In the gloom he thought he'd seen movement so stepped forward to let his eyes adjust to the darkness.

'Mr Bainbridge?' he shouted again. 'I'd just like to talk to you for a few minutes. I'm not from the police.' On both sides were enormous uneven walls of hay bales. He thought he'd seen a shape at the top of one of them so he continued into the barn. Suddenly the hay stack to his right swayed and started to move. Too late. He began to back up as heavy bricks of hay came crashing down around him. One struck him on the back, and he felt a burst of pain from his shoulder as he fell, and more bales piled up on him. Stunned, he tried to move, but his arm was hurting too much, and the tremendous weight on his body was starting to crush the air out of him. He was trapped, and panic began to grip his lungs in the dusty gloom. A rectangle of hay seems like such an innocuous thing when you see it lying in a field or you are sitting drinking cider on one, and it was ridiculous to think you could be killed by them. But there was a very real possibility this wasn't going to end well. The pockets created by the angles of the bales were all that were protecting him from the full crush, and a sudden movement might shift the weight enough to make it fatal.

He tried to call for help, but didn't have much wind left in his lungs, and the hay was deadening his sounds. He tried to reach for his pocket where his phone was but his left hand wouldn't move at all and his right was wedged between two bales. He could feel the murky depths of unconsciousness beginning to swirl around him. He tried to kick his feet, but his legs were trapped. The pain in his shoulder was all that was keeping him conscious. Every time he tried to move his arm a stabbing sensation ran through him and the shock of it kept him from passing out. He lay still. He could hear his own laboured breathing but thought he heard something else too. Perhaps it was an engine, or the rumble of a tractor. He concentrated on breathing, on getting oxygen into his system. He tried again to shout, but nothing came from his throat. He could feel the pull of an old scar he had on his chest that was being stretched by his position, and he pushed it out of his mind.

After a long while, he didn't know how long, without warning, a tiny shaft of light pierced the murkiness and he could hear the grunts of someone straining with effort. He shouted for help and this time his voice emerged faintly. The bales were loosening and then after what seemed like a very long time the weights lifted from his chest and legs. He blinked the dust from his eyes and could see he was looking up at a sweaty, angry face.

'What are you doing in my barn?'

McQueen managed to sit up, but his shoulder was screaming with pain, and he let out a loud groan as his left arm lay uselessly in his lap.

'If you're Bainbridge, I came to see you,' he gasped. 'I wanted to talk to you.'

'You've dislocated your shoulder by the look of it,' said Bainbridge. With surprising gentleness, he took McQueen's arm and put his other hand on the throbbing shoulder.

'People's bones are no different from animal's,' he said, and then without warning gave the arm a tug and a twist while pushing hard on McQueen's shoulder. The pain was excruciating, and McQueen screamed loudly thinking he would pass out. Then suddenly the pain stopped and was replaced by a dull ache. He moved his arm. It was working again. McQueen wasn't entirely convinced his orthopaedic make up was the same as a sheep or horse, but the shoulder did feel better.

'You could've gone to the hospital,' said the farmer, nodding at the arm. 'They'd give you injections and x-rays. It would all take much longer and the result's the same. Plus there would have been questions about how it happened and the last thing I need is more attention from health and safety. You were trespassing and it's your own fault, but they wouldn't listen to me.'

'Thank you,' said McQueen. 'I think you saved my life.'

'Why were you climbing on them?' he asked, still

The Murder Option

angry and pointing at the wall. 'It'll take me hours to put all these back.'

'I wasn't. I was down here. I thought you were in here. I called out and then they fell.'

'They didn't fall. Someone must have pushed them. They were stacked safe. I drove in the yard and lucky for you I saw your car. Then I saw the barn door was open. I could see some of the hay through the gap so I thought there might be someone under here. Good job for you I did.'

'Could any of your workers have been in here and knocked them accidentally?'

'No one's in today. I can only afford to use casuals when I need them, and I haven't got any on the farm at the moment. It was your fault. You shouldn't have been in here, so don't make out it's my fault. This is a working farm.'

'You're right,' said McQueen, rubbing his shoulder and grimacing. 'I take total responsibility. Don't worry.'

Bainbridge helped McQueen up and then took him across the yard to his house. They sat in the messy kitchen, but there were no offers of tea.

Bainbridge wasn't one for small talk. 'Why are you here? Are you a reporter?'

'No, my name's McQueen. I'm a private investigator, and I'm trying to help Mrs Baxter, the wife of the dead man you found on your land.'

Bainbridge threw up his hands and started to get very angry again.

'Not this again. I told the police everything. I know I shouldn't have moved him, but I didn't kill him. He was dead when I found him.' McQueen didn't want another

54

disastrous interview, especially as it had nearly killed him to get this one, so he moved quickly to reassure the old farmer.

'Mr Bainbridge, I know that, and I'm not saying you did, I just want to know if you saw anything near the body when you first picked it up? I'm really looking for anything that might give me a new clue, any evidence the police might have overlooked while they were trying to pin it on you.'

The farmer shook his head. 'I don't want anything to do with this. It's over, and if I'd known you were coming I'd have locked the gate.'

McQueen was still feeling shaken by his ordeal, but he managed to sound soothing,

'Okay, Mr Bainbridge, I understand how you feel, but there are two things I'd like to say to you,' he said, trying a different tack. 'You were pretty badly treated by the police and the press. I know that. You probably don't feel very charitable towards them, but this isn't about helping them. It's about showing them what a bad job they've done. They need to be taught a lesson, wouldn't you say? If I can get some proof against a murderer, something they haven't found, it's going to be very embarrassing for them. Also, it would put to bed forever the idea that you had anything to do with it.'

Bainbridge shrugged.

'So what? People believe what they want to believe.'

'And the other thing,' said McQueen pushing on, 'is that body you found wasn't just a bag of spuds, it was a human being and Mrs Baxter lost her husband. He might have been an inconvenience to you, but he was the love of her life, and she'd like to see some justice done.'

The Murder Option

The farmer was unmoved.

'He was no innocent,' said Bainbridge.

'What do you mean?'

'I read the papers, too. He worked for that engineering firm, and they were the ones I caught fly-tipping on my field last year. I took pictures of their lorry and I got my solicitor to prosecute them, but they wiggled out of it by blaming it on subcontractors. But it was them.'

'Wait a minute. So, you're saying Harper Engineering had been fly-tipping before on your land?'

'That's right.'

'So that connects someone in Harper's firm with the field the body was dumped in?'

'I don't know about that. All I know is they're all crooks. They're the ones dumping rubbish on my field, but I'm the one who ends up getting fined.'

Twelve

McQueen's shoulder ached like hell, but the two paracetamols combined with the comforting anaesthetic of alcohol was starting to take the edge off the pain. Shirtless, he looked at himself in the bathroom mirror and at the ugly bruising that had already spread part way across his chest. For once ignoring the old purple scar on his chest, he rotated his arm gingerly. At least he could still move it, and he'd managed to drive home. He took a bag of peas from the freezer and, sitting on the sofa with a wince, he awkwardly taped the icy package to his shoulder before taking another glug of red.

Not for the first time he shook his head as he contemplated his situation. The conclusion was inescapable. He was an idiot. Yes, he'd gained a good degree in psychology, followed by a Masters in Forensic Psychology and then crawled his way word by word to a hard-won Ph.D. in Criminology. His impressive qualifications were a testament to many years of sacrifice, of parties and gatherings missed, of thousands of hours of studying and slaving over books, and the mind-numbing stress of taking exam after exam. It had been the most valuable education, all aimed at teaching him something about how a mind works, and yet somehow he'd managed to be so stupid as to end up here, bruised, battered and sitting in his living room, lucky to be alive. He knew that in his old life he could have spent the day quietly marking coursework for eager students keen to gain his approval or delivering one of his impressive lectures to a sea of spell-bound young faces. He could still be doing those things were it not for, amongst other things, the haunting feeling of dissatisfaction that had infused his academic life. It had started as a sneaking hunch that what he did was worthless in the scheme of things and had, over time, become a strong urge to do something more meaningful. Something where he could actually help living, breathing people rather than endlessly theorising about how they became corpses. There had been other influences too, more graphic personal reasons which had meant the urge had grown and become an obsession that had ultimately stolen his comfortable, ordered life to replace it with this chaos.

'What the hell is going on?' he yelled at the wall.

One of the downsides of always working alone was that he didn't have anyone to bounce his thoughts and profanities off, so he tended to talk aloud to himself or bash away at his laptop as if it were a confidante. Focus on the case, he told himself, concentrate on the now and push away the doubts.

He ran the mental film of the day over again in his head. If the bales hadn't just accidentally fallen, then someone had pushed them down on top of him, and it meant someone wanted to hurt him enough to get him off the case. But who? No one knew he was going to the farm unless someone had been following him. The only people who seemed to be upset he had taken on the investigation were Harper and the police. But if the avalanche of hay had been meant to put him off, it had done the opposite. Now he was sure there was something to find.

The case against Martin Harper engineering magnate was building up, especially now his firm could be linked to the farmer's field, but there was still not a shred of real evidence. And there was something about the way Valerie Baxter had been so unflinchingly sure Harper was the culprit that rankled with him, especially now it might be true they'd had a history she'd failed to mention.

What McQueen needed now was to have a discussion with his employer. She needed to tell him the truth, and he needed to lay out some ground rules. But that was a task for tomorrow, and what he really needed right now was rest and recuperation, otherwise known as another drink.

When they'd first got married, he and Julie had joked a lot about the 'in sickness or in health' part of the vows. They both agreed that the health would be easy, but the sickness part might be a challenge. And so it had proved. Right now, McQueen could have done with someone to run a bath for him and then tuck him up in bed with a hot drink. He was feeling sore and sorry for himself, and not for the first time he grudgingly allowed himself to admit that alcohol couldn't fulfil all the functions of a good and trusted friend.

He took the makeshift icepack from his shoulder and

threw it onto the coffee table. If anything, the cold was making the pain worse.

One of his nagging concerns regarding the case was that he had no real sense of Colin Baxter. He'd read the police reports. They had looked carefully into his financial and personal background, but found nothing unusual or suspicious that could have explained his murder. Everyone McQueen had asked about the victim had been at pains to stress that he was a nice man. Once again it all led round in the same tired circle to the same conclusion, that the only person who appeared to have any kind of possible motive to thrust a knife through his heart was Harper.

There was the other troubling theory, however, the one Anne Kirkpatrick had touched on, and it was too frustrating to contemplate at the moment. Random stranger killings were notoriously difficult to resolve. Without clear connections, they usually relied on the murderer being caught for something else, and then traced back to the crime. But this didn't feel random to McQueen. Opportunist murderers didn't usually kidnap active, middle-aged men in the middle of the day to kill them, but if that is what had happened here, then they would probably never find the answer.

Thirteen

Valerie Baxter's house was not what McQueen had expected. It wasn't the pristine palace he'd imagined from her neat personality and dress sense, or the ordered neatness of her brother's house. Valerie's was a medium-sized suburban semi-detached in one of the affluent outskirts of Leeds that had at least three houses' worth of old furniture and cheap ornaments stuffed into it. It wasn't quite a chaotic hoarder's house, as seen on so many TV shows, there was no discarded rubbish or food anywhere, but it was still an example of compulsive hoarding. It was relatively clean, but there was just too much unneeded furniture, too much clashing art on the walls, too many ornaments stacked against walls, just too much stuff. He recognised the classic hallmarks of a person who has a problem letting go of anything, and it fitted well with her pursuit of Harper's conviction.

When they were sitting down, each on their own facing couch, in the small room with four couches in it, their knees were almost touching. McQueen was about to start the chat,

The Murder Option

but Valerie beat him to it by asking if he had spoken to Martin Harper yet. With some irritation he barely managed to hide, he waved away her question. He needed to set the tone here. Sitting in these intimate cluttered surroundings, McQueen was struck again by the disarming, unwavering stare from Valerie's shingly pretty eyes. It was certainly possible that Harper had been attracted to her, and with a husband quite a lot older than her it was also possible she had succumbed to the well-preserved and energetic man of power.

'Mrs Baxter,' he said. 'If I'm going to continue with this case I need to make a few things clear. Firstly, I need you to be totally honest with me at all times, otherwise it can start to get a little confusing and I can end up chasing my own tail.'

'I have been honest,' she said evenly.

McQueen nodded. 'The other thing I need to make clear is my job is to find your husband's killer. It's not to frame Martin Harper no matter whether the evidence supports that point of view or not. Harper may well turn out to be guilty. He certainly looks like a favourite candidate at the moment, but I have to be open to all possibilities, otherwise we could end up with an unsupportable case. Do you understand?'

'But he did do it,' she said. 'And if you speak to him, you'll see that.'

Pleasant as she was, McQueen was getting tired of her one-track mind.

'I have spoken to him, and although he wasn't very cooperative, it doesn't make him a killer, not in the eyes of any court in this land anyway.'

'Keep looking,' she said, no emotion registering on her

face. 'You'll find the evidence.'

She was entrenched and intransigent, her hard centre showing again, so McQueen decided to toss a hand grenade into their cosy chat.

'Can you tell me if it's true that you had an affair with Martin Harper?' He'd expected her to bluster and immediately deny the claim, but she just stared back at him.

'Did he tell you that?'

'No, it wasn't him, but is it true?'

'Why does it matter?' That was an affirmative answer in itself.

'Because if it is true, and we ever get to court with a case against Harper, the fact you may have been in a relationship with him would make this evidence gathering look like a bitter vendetta. A defence barrister would leap on it, so it's just something I need to know going in.'

She sighed wearily.

'Yes, it is true,' she said. 'It was a very bad mistake a little while ago, and I deeply regret it, but that's not why I want justice for Colin.'

'And did your husband know about the affair?'

'Yes, he did.' She sat still, her hands intertwined on her lap. She wasn't fidgeting nervously as he might have expected.

'And what did he think about that?' prodded McQueen.

'He was upset when he found out. He loved me very much and he was hurt, but he was a very forgiving man, and he had forgiven me.'

'Really? But had he forgiven Harper?'

'I don't know if he ever spoke to him about it, but I do

The Murder Option

think it was the reason Colin wanted to leave the company, so yes, it probably was why they stopped getting on.'

There was a lull while McQueen made some notes. As usual, he was recording the conversation, but still jotted down thoughts as they occurred. Valerie spoke again.

'You went to see my brother,' she said. 'He rang and told me.'

'Yes. I was trying to get some background about Colin. He doesn't seem as convinced as you are about Harper.'

'I love my brother, he is a brilliant man, and I don't know what I would do without him, but sometimes he can't see what's right in front of his nose.'

'Okay,' said McQueen, closing his notebook with a slap. 'I'm going to keep working on this case. I think there's something here worth chasing, as long as you are aware that it's not going to be a Martin Harper witch hunt.'

'As I said,' she smiled, 'keep looking, and I'm sure you'll find what you need.'

He had chosen not to tell Valerie Baxter the main reason he wanted to pursue the case was because there seemed to be someone who didn't want him to. He also hadn't mentioned the specifics of the barn avalanche, even though his shoulder was still achingly reminding him with every move of his arm. He didn't want to alarm her especially as it might turn out to have been no more than an innocent accident, although he strongly doubted that. He was finding the close surroundings to be slightly claustrophobic and he was keen to get going but he still had a couple of questions, although he was certain he already knew the answer to the first one.

'Can you think of anyone else who may have had even

the slightest reason to kill your husband, maybe from years ago even?'

As he'd expected, the reply was unequivocal.

'No. Not one. Everyone liked Colin. He was kind and decent and a wonderful husband. He made time for everyone. I've still got the sympathy cards,' she said pointing vaguely in the direction of one of the sideboards. 'I had nearly a hundred. Beautiful messages. Do you want to see them?'

'That won't be necessary at the moment,' said McQueen, but he made a note that it might be worthwhile to trawl through them at some point to gain some names.

'One other thing,' he continued. 'I'm curious. How did you get all those police reports? It's not usual for them to release that information, even to family members.'

'You're right. I had to fight tooth and nail for them. I rang every day and I think one day I happened to get a fairly junior person who said they'd send me a report, but made the mistake of sending me the whole file. I think I was making such a fuss and threatening to go to the press that someone decided to prove how much work they had done on the case to shut me up. Fools. Actually it proves the opposite, they didn't even speak to the murderer. When the senior people found out I had the files they came to get them back but I'd already copied them.'

As he was about to stand up, McQueen's phone rang, and glancing at the screen, he saw it was Peter Bainbridge's number.

'I need to take this. It's about this case,' he said to Valerie.

'Hello?' growled Bainbridge into his ear.

The Murder Option

'Hi. How can I help you, Mr Bainbridge?'

McQueen was looking at Valerie Baxter and he could tell she recognised the name.

'I told you I've got no wish to help the police,' he said abruptly. 'But if you found the real murderer, maybe everyone would leave me alone once and for all.

'Yes, they would,' said McQueen. 'That's what I was trying to tell you.'

'Anyway, I remembered something about the morning and the top field. The wind blows hard up that field right into the hedge at the top, so I went to have another look. You come over here this afternoon, three o'clock, and I'll show you.' And then he hung up.

McQueen studied Valerie Baxter's expectant face, the pleading hope shining from her eyes. He felt the need to give her some good news, also to show he was earning his fee.

'That was the farmer who found your husband's body,' he explained. 'No one has shown him much interest. They were all too busy trying to stitch him up, but it sounds like he might have something for me. Something about a hedge. Maybe it's a break.'

'You trust him? He may not have killed my husband, but he didn't show much respect for my Colin's body, did he? And he distracted the police from Martin Harper.'

The painful emotion in her words made McQueen pause for a second. She was absolutely right. He had made the professional error of letting Baxter become 'the corpse' in his mind, forgetting that to this woman he wasn't just part of a logic puzzle, a brain teaser to be worked out, affair or no affair. He was still the man she had loved.

'You're right,' said McQueen quietly. 'But if he can help me catch your husband's murderer, maybe he can redeem himself.' He looked at the cluttered sideboard at his elbow. On it, stacked in rows, was a plethora of framed photographs. 'Is this Colin?' he asked pointing at one of the pictures of Valerie sitting laughing next to a grey-haired older man.

Show some interest, he thought.

'Yes,' she said, smiling at a memory. 'In the garden, on our anniversary. And you know him,' she said, tapping the image at the person standing behind Colin. 'That's my brother, Michael.'

It was a much younger Michael with long blond locks rather than the short brown crop he'd seen the day before. He was almost unrecognisable. Very familiar, but almost a different person.

'Gosh, he's changed,' said McQueen.

'Haven't we all?' she responded, the smile dropping from her face as her eyes began to shine with tears.

Fourteen

McQueen had expected the farm gate, sign and all, to be open as before, but it was padlocked now with a heavy chain, so he left his car and clambered over it. He shouted for Bainbridge just as he had on his first visit and, as before, received no answer. His shoulder gave an involuntary twinge as he walked past the barn he'd been trapped in. He was in no hurry to go back inside. The tractor was standing in the yard so he knew Bainbridge wasn't out working in the fields. Surely he couldn't have forgotten he was coming, it was him who had specified the time. He assumed he must be waiting in the house for him, so he crossed to the kitchen door, knocked, and then entered.

Peter Bainbridge was waiting in the kitchen, but he was not in any fit state to say hello or give McQueen any information. He was slumped back on one of the kitchen chairs, the back of his head was missing and a double-barrelled shotgun was lying on the floor at his feet. There was no way he was still alive, and there was nothing to be done for the poor man.

McQueen had seen one or two dead bodies before, but it was still a shock to see a person he had spoken to only hours earlier gone forever, his life essence pushed out through a huge hole in the back of his skull. In a strange way, he hoped that breath-taking jolt of death always stayed with him, he never wanted to reach a point where such a sight became a meaningless routine. He was still at the door and without moving further into the room he looked around as much as he could. Behind the dead man, on the surface of the cooker, and on the floor, were spread the remains of his brains. Some small flecks had also hit the wall. The gun must have been in his mouth, which was now a bloody mess from what McQueen could see from his position. He'd have needed to move the dead man's head to get a good look, and he certainly wasn't going to touch the body before it had been photographed. There was no sign of a note on the table, but a mug was lying on its side, a pool of coffee on the surface imitating the pool of blood on the floor. One of the other kitchen chairs was lying on its side, perhaps he'd kicked out in a death spasm.

Trying to carefully retrace his steps so as not to disturb any evidence, McQueen backed out of the room. Standing again in the yard, he took a deep breath. His mind was already whirring through possibilities. He knew the stats for suicide by farmers and how common it was. An isolated life, constant financial pressure and reliance on unpredictable weather along with easy access to lethal methods were all given as contributory factors to the numbers currently running at about one a week in the UK. Bainbridge had the

The Murder Option

added pressure of being labelled the idiot who, at best moved a dead body, and at worst provided it.

Although he knew all the facts and figures, McQueen was aware it meant a farmer's murder made to look like a suicide wasn't going to be questioned too much. Bainbridge had not been suicidal when he'd spoken to him, and although depressed people can be good at masking their intentions, there was no reason for him to call McQueen at all if he didn't have something important to share about the case. If the killer knew he'd found something it might be worth them bumping him off, too? As far as McQueen was concerned, the farm had already seen an attempt on his own life. He looked around the dusty yard for any signs of movement, and listened hard, but stopped himself from going to the barn. He knew he couldn't delay any longer, his first move had to be to call the police. There would be some interesting questions to answer and he'd have to give a full statement, but Bainbridge might have a family somewhere and they'd need to be told as soon as possible. He didn't want a relative turning up out of the blue and witnessing what he'd just seen. Leaning against the side of his car, slightly shaken, he looked across again at the barn where he had almost met his own demise if it hadn't had been for Bainbridge coming to his rescue. First Colin, then nearly him, and now the farmer. This place had an affinity with death, it seemed. He took his phone from his pocket and wearily dialled 999.

Fifteen

A witness statement wouldn't normally have taken very long to complete. It was just a matter of putting down on paper what you saw, having some of the finer points clarified, and then signing it. But it wasn't like that for McQueen. He was questioned for more than three hours in a dingy police interview room by a sour-faced Detective Sergeant Brooks and his colleague. There was no sensitivity shown in acknowledging any after-effects from the trauma, so it was a good job he wasn't feeling any. It seemed they weren't big fans of McQueen's work, even though they had never met him before. He guessed his reputation had preceded him, and not in a good way.

Brooks wasn't happy that McQueen had been poking his nose into the case, even after being advised not to, and he wasn't happy Bainbridge seemed to have had something to tell him. On top of whatever the farmer's evidence was, it might have been something the police had overlooked. In short, he wasn't a happy detective. His mood probably hadn't been helped by the crack McQueen had made at the start of the interview. McQueen had sarcastically pointed out that the last time someone found a body in the Baxter case, the finder had been Bainbridge. Sadly, it had led to him being wrongly charged with murder and now he was dead, so McQueen joked he was hoping for a slightly better outcome this time.

DS Brooks wasn't quite ready to officially call it a suicide, there were still lab reports to come back and a coroner's inquiry, but McQueen could tell from the way the copper was talking that the case was already closed in his eyes. In some ways that was good; at least McQueen wasn't being arrested just yet, but at the same time, if Bainbridge had been murdered to silence him, the culprit was home free. But not on McQueen's ledger.

They eventually let him go home but with all the usual caveats of making himself available for further questioning if the need should arise, and another warning to stay away from the Baxter case.

He went straight back to his office and captured every detail he could remember about finding Bainbridge, much more than he had shared with the police. He wanted to get it all down, not just the facts, he wanted the colour and feel of it while it was fresh. He started to wonder how much luck he'd have finding the field that Bainbridge had wanted to show him, but as he didn't know what he'd be looking for he wasn't sure that was such a good idea.

It was true that it could have been suicide. It certainly looked like it from the outside. Perhaps finally sick of being pointed at for Baxter's death, it might have all become too much for him, and McQueen's questions might have been the last straw. That could have been it, but that simply didn't sit right with McQueen. Bainbridge was a stubborn donkey, a guy who had fought through and come out the other side of the accusations, and McQueen couldn't see him ever giving in to that kind of pressure. He had seemed very eager on the phone to show McQueen whatever it was he had remembered, like he had a purpose, and McQueen had felt he was getting on board with the idea of finding the true murderer.

McQueen was craving a glass of red, but for that very reason he didn't keep any in the office. There was an overriding fact that he was trying to ignore, but like a rubber ball in a pond it kept surfacing no matter how much he tried to push it down. He turned over to new blank page in his note book and wrote, *The only person who knew I was going there was Valerie Baxter*.

He closed his laptop and picked up his book. He decided to call it a day. It was time to go home. Home where the wine was.

Sixteen

It was a different pub from the last time and had a very different vibe, too. When McQueen had received a call from his journalist contact, Anne Kirkpatrick, to arrange another lunch meeting, he'd thought it would be so she could quiz him about finding Peter Bainbridge. He'd imagined she'd try to get some background on what could be a juicy story, but right from the off he could tell this meeting was different. For a start, they stood at the bar instead of finding a table, and unbelievably she ordered a Diet Coke. McQueen didn't. It already felt as if it might be the sort of meeting that needed some alcoholic support.

She didn't waste any time getting down to business.

'I just wanted you to know it's nothing personal,' she said. 'We've had a mutually beneficial working relationship I think,' she continued, sipping her drink with a slight grimace aimed at the coke not at him. 'You know you can trust me, but I've been under some pressure from my editor.' She delved into her bag and placed a folded newspaper on the bar in front of him. He picked it up, read the headline, and scanned the story. He was famous.

He could see what was happening, the gruesome suicide of a local farmer had become a blame game, and McQueen was the villain. The police, probably worried they could be implicated for their original inept and mistaken persecution and arrest of Bainbridge, had let a mud-slinging story leak out. Clearly, the mud had been aimed at McQueen. According to the paper's version, after badgering an innocent company director to the point of having a restraining order served, McQueen had then driven Bainbridge to suicide in a one-man crusade against the innocent. It wasn't quite as clearly stated as that, but the couched accusations were low on subtlety and high on outrage, click-bait for the online edition to get the keyboard warriors indignantly firing messages across cyber-space.

McQueen read on with a humourless smile. It was quite a long piece and used some of the knowledge that Anne had gleaned about him over the years. Hypocritically, it mentioned his red wine-fuelled investigations, he snorted, this from a gin and tonic-fuelled journo. The piece ended on a call to start a national campaign to have private investigators licensed and regulated by the police. It was a good old-fashioned hatchet job, and McQueen was under the sharp blade.

He shrugged. 'You could have spoken to me first. I would have given you a different view.'

'I didn't choose the angle,' she said. 'And the source was quite well-respected.'

'I can imagine who that was. A certain DS Brooks, if I had

The Murder Option

to guess, but it doesn't matter now. It's all vague enough to be legally supportable I suppose, and you're just doing your job, right?'

'Very big of you,' said Anne. 'But I'd hang in there, McQueen. You know how short the news cycle is these days. Everything is forgotten in minutes.' McQueen wasn't quite so sure about that, but he wasn't overly concerned.

'Could cause me some reputational damage, make a few potential clients nervous, but I suppose that's the aim. It might back-fire on you, though, like the way people will always choose a bastard for a lawyer to fight their corner over a timid pushover. Clients like an investigator, even if they are unlicensed, who's willing to stir up some action and make some waves.' He was making light of it, but was disappointed that he'd never again feel comfortable with Anne Kirkpatrick within earshot.

Anne pushed aside her unfinished drink and said she had to get back to the office. She'd only met him because she wanted him to know, face to face from her, that he was today's press punch bag.

'What if I told you it might not have been suicide?' said McQueen. 'Would that be a story?' Anne stopped in her tracks. Now she was smiling.

'You know it would, so what you got?' Her eyes were bright, and he could tell the smell of a scoop was tingling her nostrils.

'For that,' said McQueen, draining his glass in one long gulp, 'you'll just have to wait.' And then throwing the rolled-up newspaper into the small puddle of lager on the bar he left.

Seventeen

McQueen walked back to his flat from the pub. He was always very careful about getting behind the wheel when he'd been in a bar or pub because he could never trust himself to know how much he'd drunk. Today he was especially glad he'd made the decision not to risk it when he saw his two favourite policemen arrive within seconds of him reaching his front door. While a drink-driving charge would have been a huge and enjoyable bonus for them, it would have been a difficult hurdle for McQueen and his need to get around for his business.

'How can I help you?' he asked the smug looking copper, but he didn't open his front door for them. He put his keys back in his pocket.

'Can we come in?' asked the shaven-headed law enforcer.

'Nope. No need,' said McQueen. 'Let's talk out here.' The cop looked at his young companion who raised his eyes to the heavens and shook his head like a toddler's

The Murder Option

disappointed parent.

'If that's what you want,' said the leader. 'We've just come to say that after recent reports in the paper we will be standing ready to follow up on any official complaints levelled at you by Mr Peter Bainbridge's family.'

'Okay,' said McQueen coolly. 'You were onto that very quickly, almost as if you knew it was coming.'

'Just so you fully understand, Mr McQueen, I'm saying I will personally make sure any complaints are pursued as far as they can go and could end up as a charge of witness harassment.'

The game here was not to show the cop that he was at all flustered or worried by the threats.

'Thank you for the information, officer,' said McQueen with a pleasant smile, as if he was thanking a friend for telling him what time the football was on. The policeman wasn't getting the reaction he'd wanted so he pushed his round head a little closer to McQueen's face as he had done before.

'I warned you not to stick your nose into this, but you didn't listen, did you? And now an innocent man is dead.'

'Good point,' said McQueen. 'The same innocent man the police wrongly accused of murder, as I remember. On the back of that he was hounded and vilified and perhaps it all became too much for him? Who knows?' He winked cheekily at the young police constable. 'Remember, there's more than one newspaper in the world,' he added. 'And other publications might see it all quite differently. What was your name again, officer?'

Once the policemen had driven away, McQueen opened

his front door. He'd put on a classy show of insouciance in the face of blatant intimidation, but knew he'd be better off without the scrutiny of the police. If they dug around long enough they were bound to catch him on something. 'Thank you so much, Anne,' he uttered under his breath.

Inside his flat he threw his keys onto the kitchen work surface. It was early, but not too early to continue the pub vibe and continue to oil his thought processes with a drop more red wine. McQueen had a system by which he drank good, expensive wine early on in the evening, but by the time it was going down like water he moved on to cheap gut-rot. It was a way of not wasting decent wine when it no longer mattered, and he was quietly proud of the economy and logic of his approach. He was still on the good stuff at the moment. With glass in hand, he went through to the lounge where he flopped onto the couch. The policemen hadn't bothered him unduly, they were only trying to scare him away, and that had to mean pressure was being rolled downhill to them. That was a message in itself, someone further up the chain had an interest in this murder being forgotten.

What was bothering McQueen more was the shape of this case. An honest, decent working man had been murdered and the way it was heading, no one would ever be charged. Meanwhile a devastated widow was left to face the future with nothing but questions. Even if Harper didn't turn out to be the culprit it would still be better for her to know what had really happened than to spend her days in the dungeon of ignorance. It brought to mind a concept he'd played around with for a long time.

The Murder Option

He lay back on the sofa and thought about the contours and colours of the perfect murder. The commonly accepted belief, and McQueen had heard it a lot, was that there was no such thing as a perfect murder. It was nonsense, of course. Perfect murders were the ones that, by their very nature, were never discovered, and they were probably happening all the time. Several infamous serial killers such as Dennis Nilsen, the scourge of the hidden gay community in North London during the eighties, had committed numerous perfect murders that could have gone undetected and unpunished forever. His mistake was to move to Muswell Hill, keep on murdering and then block up the drains with body parts. But the concept of the perfect murder was a fascination for a lot of students, and McQueen had once set a lecture topic and paper on the subject. As an introduction, he'd given them an example of his own.

In McQueen's version of a perfect murder, the only ingredients he needed were a small sailing boat he could handle without a crew, and his unsuspecting victim. The target was probably a tiresome family member, a rich wife or husband, and under the guise of a wonderful holiday they would sail far out to sea. The murder would take place a long way from shore and away from curious eyes, the body thrown overboard afterwards, never to be found.

No witnesses, no body, no one to prove that a tragic sailing accident hadn't occurred. People went missing from boats all the time, and there was no way of knowing how many of them were murders, certainly none that could be proved.

It was a slightly tongue in cheek example because

McQueen couldn't sail and he hated being on boats, the enormity and power of the sea terrified him, but the key components of the perfect murder were all there. No witnesses, no body, no evidence and even strongest suspicion would never get you into court. He wasn't sure why he was thinking about that particular lecture right at that moment. It had popped into his head unbidden.

He stood up and started to pace around his living room. He wanted to map out a possible scenario that could work. He began talking out loud.

'Baxter can't stand being around Harper anymore because of his history with Valerie, so he decides to leave the company. More than that, he wants revenge for the affair, so he threatens to take a few secrets over to a competitor. He tells Harper and they have an all-out row in the office that's overheard by my anonymous woman. That's when there's all the talk of back stabbing. Then what? Baxter doesn't leave the firm immediately because he's negotiating something, perhaps. Blackmailing, maybe. At that point, for some reason, maybe his fear of the secrets, Harper decides his only way out is to take the murder option. He ambushes Baxter on his way to work. But no witnesses have come forward to say they saw him that morning, no one saw him getting into a car and CCTV doesn't show him getting on the train, either. He takes him somewhere, stabs him in the back, and brings the body to the field. He chooses the field, why? Is it the only place he can think of? But why be so obvious about it? Why not try to hide the body or at least try to make it look like an accident? But then he has a stroke of luck, Bainbridge moves the body and becomes suspect number one, while Harper's family connection makes sure the police have no interest in him.'

McQueen slumped back down onto the sofa. As a scenario it was possible, for sure, but there were things about it which didn't ring true. For a calculating, self-made millionaire businessman, it was a hell of a risky option. And if it had happened like that then where was the evidence going to come from? It could only come from Harper himself and, right now, McQueen couldn't get near him. He needed to find a way to winkle him out, to put him under more pressure and hope he let something slip.

He was about to turn on the TV to get some mindless distraction in the hope that a break from thinking about the case would help, when his phone rang. It was a male voice.

'Is that Mr McQueen, the private investigator?'

'Yes. Who's this?'

'My name's David Bainbridge. Peter Bainbridge was my father.' There was an awkward pause. 'It says in the paper that you drove my father to commit suicide.'

McQueen closed his eyes and grimaced. He had the option of putting the phone down, but the man deserved better than that.

'I'm sorry about your father, David, I truly am. And I know what they've said, but you shouldn't believe everything you read.'

'I don't.' It was a short definite response that sounded like the son had inherited his father's abruptness. 'My father never committed suicide,' he continued. 'They've forgotten about God,' he said defiantly.

'God?' It wasn't often that McQueen heard the big man

used as a character witness, and he was intrigued.

'Yes, they never knew my father, but he was a religious man, a true believer. He thought suicide was a sin against God.' McQueen wasn't sure how Bainbridge would have explained moving Colin Baxter's lifeless body to God, but he wasn't about to get into that.

'He would have clung onto life until the last,' continued his son. 'He was a fighter, and he rang me that very morning to tell me he had spoken to you. He said you were giving him a chance to fight back against the police. He was excited, well as excited as he ever got.'

When he'd said he was the farmer's son, McQueen had expected to be fending off foul-mouthed threats based on the negative press coverage, so the turn in direction took him slightly by surprise. The professional in him knew it was an opportunity not to be squandered.

'Can I ask you, David, if your father had any history of depression or mental illness?'

'No, never. I mean, he could be a mad bugger sometimes, but I don't think that's what you mean.'

It was going to sound a bit strange to David, but while he had him on the phone, McQueen needed to ask about the field.

'And I'm sorry if this is painful, but I need to know. On the day he died, he said he had something to show me in the top field. Did he tell you what it was?'

'No, I'm afraid not. But the reason I'm ringing is I will be giving my evidence to the coroner, but the police have already told me they think it's suicide. A liaison officer tried to tell me that often family members are shocked by a death

The Murder Option

like this because they never saw it coming. She said they often feel guilty about not spotting the signs.'

'Well, those things are true, David, in some cases, but in this case you shouldn't feel guilty. It was nothing to do with you,' offered McQueen. There was a snort from the other end of the line.

'I don't feel guilty. Me and the old man might not have seen eye to eye all the time, but I know this, he didn't top himself. That's why I want to hire you.'

'What?'

'You're an investigator, aren't you? I think the police and the coroner are going to whitewash this and close the book on this as quickly as they can, but I want someone to find out what really happened. You met him, you know what he was like.'

McQueen didn't say anything, and David mistook the silence for reticence.

'I'll pay the going rate,' he added, 'if that's what you're worried about.'

It was the chance to get paid double for the same job, and McQueen knew his accountant would be grinning at the prospect, but it wasn't the way McQueen operated. It was his turn to give a dismissive sound into the phone.

'David, you don't need to hire me and you don't have to pay me anything. I'm on this case now even if no one pays me. If I can find out what happened to your dad, I will. He saved my life, I owe him.'

'He never mentioned that?'

'Of course he didn't. He didn't think it was anything special, but there was an incident in his barn, maybe an accident, maybe not, but I got buried, and he pulled me out. I have to be honest with you, David, I owe you that. It could turn out that if I hadn't started poking around none of this might have happened. I've stirred up some ghosts and your dad might have been a victim of that.' There was another longish pause, and McQueen wasn't sure how it was going to end, but he'd felt duty bound to make the young man aware of how this could pan out.

'Can't change what's happened,' said David eventually. 'The old man always made his own decisions, and you couldn't have made him do anything he didn't want to do. The main thing now for the hereafter and for the future is to keep suicide off that death certificate.'

Eighteen

McQueen may not have been taking on any new cases while he grappled with the Baxter murder, but it didn't mean the admin generated by the old jobs had become any less daunting while he'd been neglecting it. It was the ever-present eighty-twenty rule that plagued his life. Eighty percent of the work was done in twenty percent of the time, but the final excruciating twenty percent took eighty percent of his soul away with it. There were some invoice reminders to send and plenty of bills to pay, too, so he went into his office to see if he could make a dent in the choking weight of unwelcome correspondence. He turned on the computer and opened his accounts spreadsheet but struggled to concentrate on the columns of figures. He looked at the top entry, the only bright spot. It reminded him that he hadn't heard from Grace in a while. She was an elderly woman who needed McQueen's professional attention for her grandson from time to time. If Grace didn't need him anymore that had to be a good thing for her and her family, it meant things were going well. Unfortunately, it was also a very bad thing for McQueen's credit column if the regular cash injections were to stop.

It was no good. Numbers were just numbers, and the darkness of his past was gnawing at him again. He found himself thinking about his first unofficial case, still unsolved and haunting him after all these years. It was the one which had dragged him out of his academic comfort zone and thrust him into the real world of noise and dirt. It was the one that had shown him theory only goes so far.

Marion Connolly, one of his fellow lecturers, had been killed on her way home one night. She'd been bludgeoned to death as she walked through the dark outreaches of the huge college car park. A brilliant psychology scholar, with several books to her name, she had started at the college about the same time as McQueen, and they had instantly become friends. Her background was Southern Irish. She had a wicked sense of humour, a sharply caustic tongue, and was always ready to puncture any pomposity she detected in her fellow academics or any slow-witted students. McQueen had been the target of her barbs from time to time and he knew they stung. She was a woman he'd liked and respected enormously. He'd had an emotional attachment to the bright, formidable speaker and debater, and she was someone he still thought about on an almost daily basis.

There was a lot of personal regret mixed up in McQueen's sad memories of Marion. They had become very close for a while, spending daily lunches and some after-work evenings together. A mutual bond had sparked between them and an undeniable sexual attraction fizzed

The Murder Option

around their meetings. McQueen had been transported back to his magical school days, when the thought that he would be sitting behind the lovely Sonia Parker made Monday morning double-maths not only bearable but something to be eagerly anticipated throughout a boring Sunday. It was the same with Marion. Knowing he would be able to see her for a few minutes that day made any day a brighter prospect. Even though McQueen was still married at this point, and so was Marion for that matter, on his part it was an admiration that had slipped irresistibly into wonderful infatuation. It had become overpowering, McQueen had felt his life was about to change for the better, and all he felt was excitement. But Marion was, as usual, ahead of him. She was self-aware, intelligent and principled, and one night as they sat in a wine-bar near to the college she had dealt with the unspoken potential of their relationship in her typically forthright manner.

'What two people in our situation would usually do at this point in a close friendship is have an affair,' she said looking directly at him. 'But you and I are not going to do that.'

'No,' he'd answered, unconvincingly. 'Because?'

She'd wrinkled her nose at the thought of it.

'Because it's what everyone does, McQueen. And it would ruin everything. Besides, I love my husband, and you love your wife.' He'd looked across the small, round table with its flickering candle wedged into a wax encrusted old wine bottle and thought she'd never looked lovelier. The magnetism of forbidden fruit tantalisingly out of arm's reach. Disappointment was sweeping over him in a much stronger wave than he would have expected. He hadn't quite realised how deeply he'd sunk into the warm embrace of romantic possibility. He knew there was no point arguing with her. She was right, but a fantasy had been surgically removed, leaving an instant scar.

'Yes, that's right,' he'd answered, still sounding like his full commitment wasn't backing up the words. They'd ended the evening with a gentle kiss and the understanding there were to be no more intimate dinners although public lunches in the college refectory would be allowed. They were Marion's terms, and McQueen agreed, glad to accept any chink of light, knowing she was one hundred percent right. Some of the sunshine leaked out of his working life in the following days, but much worse was to follow.

It was only a few months later that the shocking discovery of Marion's body had all but locked the campus down, and over the next few days the police had questioned everyone including, and especially, him. He had taken the news badly and had been struggling to comprehend the awful, personal loss. At first, Julie had been equally shocked and mildly supportive, having not realised the true extent of McQueen's feelings for his now dead colleague. But as time went on, his obvious distress began to make her very uncomfortable and suspicious. If she was only a work colleague, then why was he so badly affected?

He was raw and vulnerable when he'd first been taken in to be harshly quizzed by the police. Rumours had been rife in the college about the time he had been spending with Marion, and those whispers had soon reached the ears of the law. When he was asked outright if he'd had a sexual relationship with her, McQueen was able to respond honestly that he had not, but kept to himself it was her choice more than his, in case it made him sound like a guilty man scorned. She had broken his heart, perhaps, but Marion Connolly was the last person in the world he would have wished any harm on, but he didn't trust the police to understand the subtlety of their relationship. Fortunately, yes, McQueen could *account for his whereabouts sir*, during the important time slots, so he'd been dismissed, and the search went on but, ultimately, it had drawn a blank. There were appeals for information, even a TV appearance by the Chief Constable, but to no avail. The months went by. There were no suspects, and the case went cold.

Some weeks after the incident, seeing McQueen's unabating grief, Julie had asked him the same question the police had asked him and again he had been able to answer honestly that he hadn't slept with Marion.

'But did you want to? Was that it?' she asked, ever the insightful reader of his emotions. Marriage is based on honesty, they say, but McQueen lied, and perhaps that had been the beginning of the end.

It had frustrated McQueen immensely he hadn't been able to help, especially when he spoke to Marion's family, and he saw the devastation that had been caused by this one seemingly random act. Speaking to her husband had been tough, and seeing the soft-spoken, broken man whose life had been torn apart by the loss of the love of his life made McQueen realise how right Marion had been. It was after that incident he knew for sure that no amount of book work would ever make up for actually finding a killer. But he'd never managed it for Marion. He had come up with a criminal profile of what type of person the killer was likely to be and what they should be looking for and asking, but the police were not interested. It was made very clear to him they had their own profilers thank you very much, and they weren't looking for outside input.

Marion Connolly's death was the first of two life-changing events that had led to McQueen leaving the comfort of academia behind. The other was even more life-threatening and personal, but Marion's killing had certainly put the first huge tear in the fabric of the way he thought about everything. But life went on, he continued as before, and the lurid mental images of what had happened to Marion faded, although his affection for her didn't. It wasn't until two and a half years later that he'd told his wife he had decided to take a different path in his professional life, not knowing it was a path that would eventually split from hers.

McQueen was shaken from his regretful thoughts by a knock at his office door. He almost physically jumped with surprise as he rarely got unexpected visitors.

The office building was a large, converted, once-grand merchant's house now riddled with the electronic arteries of essential modern communication that the original builders of the house could never have imagined. McQueen shared the main front door with three other companies; a small independent insurance brokers, a highly acclaimed accountancy firm, and a three-person web design agency called Bantaz. They all worked on the floors above him and he saw various members of the firms infrequently in the shared hallway. Not long after moving in, McQueen had used the web designers to build his own website and he had developed a friendly relationship with the young guy, Danny, who'd built his site, but other than that he didn't have much to do with any of the others except one of the accountants whom he had done some important work for.

Each company had its own separate office door, but there was no central reception area. People could walk in off the street, although it was rare. Sometimes some of the other occupants came down to moan to McQueen about the landlord, but usually McQueen's appointments were scheduled so he didn't get many interruptions.

The young woman who came in introduced herself in a startlingly strong West Country accent as Tracey Bingham, and said she'd come about a criminal case. She was dressed casually in a sweatshirt and jeans with her light blonde hair pinched back into a severe short ponytail and she didn't look upset or tearful which most of McQueen's clients usually did when they first came in regardless of their gender. By the time a person had plucked up the courage to visit a private detective they were usually at the end of some kind of emotional or financial tether.

McQueen judged his visitor was in her early thirties, a pleasant face, she wore no make-up and she carried herself with the confidence and poise of an athlete. Her movements were easy and sure as she sat in the chair without being asked and he sensed she felt as much in control of the situation as he did. He started to explain to Tracey he was very sorry, but he wasn't able to take on any new cases at the moment. She cut him off with a raised hand.

'I'm a police detective,' she said. 'But don't worry, Mr

McQueen. Officially, I'm not here today. This is all off the record. I want to ask you about your current case, the Colin Baxter murder case, to be exact.'

McQueen was immediately suspicious, wary of some kind of trap. In his experience there was no 'off the record' with the police, but there was something genuine and disarming about this impressively energetic woman at his desk, so he chose to give her five minutes to talk while he carefully watched every word that he himself uttered. She started by telling him she had been one of the people working on the Baxter case, but then she'd been taken off of it. No reason had been given to her, but she felt it might be because she'd asked too many questions about Martin Harper.

'They may be calling it a live and active case, but you'd never know it down at the station. As far as I can see, the whole thing has been wound down,' she said. 'And I'm forbidden from spending any more time on it.'

'So why have you come to see me?'

'My concern is it will all be left to rot now and I don't want that to happen. That's why I've come here to see you. If you're still looking into this I want to give you any help I can, *but*,' she added holding up her finger to emphasise the point, 'without breaking any rules and without compromising my career.'

He was very surprised and looked more closely at her to try to assess whether she was feeding him a line. She met his gaze without blinking, and her earnest intensity certainly made her words sound plausible. If she was lying she was very good at it.

McQueen was still cautious.

'Okay, Tracey. I know why I'm working on this. I'm being paid by his wife, but why is Colin Baxter so important to you?' he asked.

She frowned like it was the stupidest question she'd ever heard.

'Because he's the victim of a deadly crime and he deserves justice. That's why I joined the police in the first place. I think there's more to know here, and I also think it could be solved. It just needs a bit of time and effort. I've made my point to my superiors, but unfortunately the people in charge don't agree.' McQueen was still mulling it over when she added, 'I was starting to think I'd have to let it go and then came Bainbridge. It's a hell of a coincidence, you start to ask questions again and he dies. I looked at the reports and I visited the scene. Everyone wants to neatly box it off as a suicide but I don't believe it.'

McQueen liked what he was hearing, but he still didn't want to show his hand too early.

'Why?' he asked. 'Maybe the papers are right, and I drove him over the edge.'

'There's lots of things that indicate it wasn't a suicide. For a start there was no note. It's not conclusive proof, but there were also several signs of a struggle.' The image of the spilled coffee flashed through McQueen's mind. 'And it was a gun that would have been very hard to reach down and fire into his own mouth,' she went on. 'Also, some of the splatter pattern was inconsistent. Shooting up from a sitting position, there shouldn't have been as much debris down on the cooker. My guess is he was shot standing up by a taller man and then put in the seated position.'

McQueen nodded. 'But won't the coroner's evidence show all that?'

'Not if they don't bother to look properly because the outcome has already been decided. For convenience, and to help everything run smoothly, they can just say it's highly probable that it was a suicide and close the case. A farmer's suicide is an easy thing to pass off.'

Tracey's energy, enthusiasm, and diligence were all impressing the hell out of McQueen. If she was really going to help him, this could be the sort of leg-up that would make all the difference. He'd never had any kind of access to the police and the possibility she might be able to give him some insight and guidance was quite thrilling. Then she hit him with it.

'So, Mr McQueen, did *you* kill him? You were the one who discovered him. Was that just a neat side-step to take you out of the frame?'

McQueen recognised the technique. He'd used it himself many times. Soften up the suspect with things they want to hear, and then try to throw them off balance with a brutal curve ball.

'No, I didn't,' he replied evenly. 'I wanted him alive. He told me he had something to share with me, and that's why he rang me to arrange the meeting. I'm sure the phone records can verify that.'

She nodded.

'They do. I didn't think for a minute you did it, you had no reason, but I wanted to ask to see your reaction.'

'So, what did you expect?' asked McQueen. 'Did you

The Murder Option

come hoping to hit the jackpot, to get a tearful confession so you could look good back at the station? Was that all?' He'd been bruised by Anne Kirkpatrick's use of him as a football and he didn't want it to happen again.

She was unruffled by the snap in his tone.

'No, McQueen. What I need to know is that there is someone actively working on the murder of Colin Baxter, and possibly Peter Bainbridge. They might be linked by more than Bainbridge being the one to find Baxter.'

'You shouldn't forget there could be totally unconnected reasons for his death. Other suspects. For instance, David Bainbridge, the son. I don't think he had a great relationship with his old man, and if he stands to inherit the farm it gives him a good motive. Funnily enough, he rang me a little while ago to ask me to look into his father's death, but that could just be to throw me off the scent?'

She was shaking her head.

'I've already thought of that and I looked into it. David doesn't inherit the farm.'

'Who does?'

'The banks. Bainbridge was up to his neck in debt, and I don't think even in these ruthless times banks are bumping off farmers for their land.'

The more he spoke to her, the more he believed Tracey Bingham was the genuine article. Intelligent, dedicated, and with a lot of integrity, the only question was why did she need him?

'Okay, so what do you want from me, Tracey?'

'I told you. I have no time and for my own peace of mind. I need to know that if I stumble across something interesting on this case, there's someone I can pass it to - someone who isn't going to ignore it and fob me off or tell me it's not worth their time.'

'And then?' asked McQueen, knowing there had to be a payoff.

'And then, if it ever gets to the stage of an arrest, I want to be the one to do it. You're right about that part,' she said, pushing away from the desk and standing up. 'I do want to look good back at the station. Ever since I transferred up here from Devon and Cornwall, I've been side-lined and ignored. The girl from the sticks with a funny accent. I need to make a bang, and I'm hoping you might deliver the gunpowder.'

Nineteen

McQueen took his favourite fountain pen and paused over the blank sheet. Usually, he used ballpoints just like everyone else for jotting down fast notes, but when it came to thinking things out, he liked the timing and flow of his old Montblanc. It had been a wedding gift from Julie, and was just about the only thing he'd kept.

They had met at university. Both studied psychology, and both had been in the same intimate tutorials. He remembered the thrill of seeing the slim, pretty Scottish girl he'd already spotted on campus standing outside the room and realising she was going to be in the same small room as him. There was eye-contact and nervous smiles, and then inside they began secretly making fun of the doddery old tutor behind his back. He'd always found that shared illicit giggles are a fast track to bonding, and he'd been instantly interested in the very lovely fellow giggler and her naughty smile. A growing affection and deep friendship between them had blossomed in their second year and had become a full-blown relationship by their third. That was by the time Julie had decided nothing better seemed to be coming along, as she liked to joke. They had got married while Julie was still pushing her way forward in her first job and McQueen was studying for his doctorate. Looking back, McQueen sometimes wondered if they had both been trying desperately to cling onto the innocence of their student years in sticking together, pathetically trying to stave off adulthood. It hadn't been easy in the beginning. Saving up was their default setting and they'd got married on impulse at a time when money was painfully short, so the gesture of the extravagant pen had been a big deal. It still was.

Very deliberately, he wrote *Martin Harper* at the top of the paper and then began mapping out what he knew.

It wouldn't be the first time he'd chased down a successful businessman. McQueen had enjoyed a particularly satisfying case when he'd caught a pilfering financial director in a large firm who'd been getting away with blaming his crimes on subordinates and watching their lives collapse while his own prospered. It was in the interview that he'd shown no human emotion at all over the subsequent fate of a single-mother ex-colleague of more than ten years that McQueen had first suspected him.

It was well known in certain branches of popular psychology that exactly the same personality traits which made some people very successful as they clawed their way to the top of large organisations were the same attributes most seen in the personality disorder known as psychopathy. Traits such as lack of empathy, zero conscience, no concept of guilt or loyalty, and the ability to see other people as mere pawns in their world, were often rewarded in some company cultures. Reckless risk-taking based on impulsiveness along with a superficial charm used as a devastating tool were also assets in some workplaces as well as commonly seen characteristics on death row of prisons in America. Most successful people weren't psychopaths, but there had been enough research to show a worrying few were. The accepted statistics put the estimated number of psychopaths in the population at around one percent. That meant in the UK there were possibly just over half a million psychopaths in circulation. Most of them weren't killers, but that left a lot of others in normal jobs.

Psychopaths were the anomaly in McQueen's argument for the gravity of the murder option. Psychopaths saw no difference between choosing killing over any other choice. To a psychopath, choosing an expedient murder solution held the same weight as choosing which pair of shoes to put on in the morning.

If Harper saw no consequences to the risk of killing his right-hand-man, had no remorse over losing an old colleague, and saw no logical reason not to remove the threat of losing information to a competitor by murder, then he might well have carried out the murder. And dumping the body in plain sight where he knew it would be found? Maybe that was some kind of warning to anyone else thinking of crossing him.

A thought occurred, and McQueen stopped writing, turned on his computer and went to the satellite maps. He located the Bainbridge farm and then scooted around it. He was in luck. There was only one field that ran alongside a small road, the one popular with fly-tippers. Surely that had to be the hedge he'd been talking about. It had been a long time now since the murder and the police lab people had already been in, but if there was something worth killing Bainbridge over it might still be there. He didn't know what he might be looking for, but it was a lead, and he didn't have a lot of those right now.

He was about to head out but reaching to pick up his jacket from the back of the chair his shoulder achingly reminded him of the barn incident. He realised it could be a good idea to have someone else with him. He looked at his pad on the desk and the contact details she'd left and phoned DC Tracey Bingham.

Twenty

He parked his car behind hers in the lane. 'I think this must be the field,' said McQueen.

'Yes, it is,' said Tracey. 'I took a look at the drawings in the file. They both climbed over the five-bar gate.

'So this is what I'm thinking. Your lab experts spent a good amount of time in the woods over there where Bainbridge moved the body.' McQueen gestured vaguely in the direction of the trees at the side of the field. 'But much less time out here. On the phone, Bainbridge mentioned the hedge, and he mentioned how windy it gets out here.' As if to underline the observation, the wind was gusting into their faces. 'So, if there had been anything out here, no matter where the body actually was, it might have blown up here and got caught in the fence.'

'Seems reasonable,' said Tracey, turning her sharp profile to face the hedge.

'So there's a chance it was missed at the time, but Bainbridge saw it and didn't want to make the same mistake and move it. I don't know what we're looking for, but it might be worth checking for anything obvious.'

They started to walk along together, their eyes scanning the dense branches and leaves. After a few steps the police detective put out an arm to stop McQueen.

'Look,' she said. He was looking but couldn't see anything in the hedge, and then he saw her squat down on her haunches to examine the ground.

'Those are fairly fresh footprints,' she said, pointing at the ridges in the mud near the bottom of the fence. 'It rained heavily the evening of Bainbridge's death, so the ground will have been soft. But it hasn't rained since.'

'Have you already checked the historical weather reports before we came out here?' asked McQueen, smiling. He already knew the answer.

'Of course,' she said matter-of-factly. 'I think someone walked along here searching just like us after the farmer's murder.' She took her phone and a tape measure from her pocket, laid the tape next to the clearest print, and took some pictures.

'It would be good to get the lab guys down here to take a cast, but unfortunately I'm on forbidden ground and I'm not even supposed to be here, so it's not going to happen.' She moved along the line and took some more images. 'So this will have to do,' she said.

'Will you send me those?' he asked.

'Yes, but I want to have a good look at them first on the computer screen.'

They walked the whole length of the hedge and found nothing else other than some ancient rotting bits of plastic bags that looked as if they had been stuck in the branches for years and an empty crisp packet so old they weren't even making that flavour anymore.

Back on the other side of the gate McQueen said, 'So what about this idea? Someone comes to see Bainbridge and uses the shotgun to threaten him into telling him what to look for in the hedge. Then he shoots him, makes it look like a suicide, and comes out to retrieve whatever it was.'

'In which case we now have the shoe size of the murderer,' said Tracey, holding up her phone. They couldn't help smiling at each other knowing something significant may have been achieved by this seemingly hopeless visit to the field. McQueen found he was enjoying the chance to sound out an idea with another person rather than to the unresponsive walls of his room. He grudgingly had to admit she'd been much more professional and observant than him, and he wasn't sure that on his own he'd have even noticed the prints.

They looked by the gate for tyre tracks, but the road was too heavily used and there was nothing to find. 'I have to get back to the station. I've been assigned a new case. One thing though,' said Tracey as she went to open her car. 'Who could have known that Bainbridge might have seen something other than you?'

'I don't know. He must have told someone else. Maybe he was excited about it and couldn't keep it to himself,' he shrugged. He wasn't ready to share his conversation with Valerie just yet. Tracey was a police officer after all and there was still no knowing where her loyalties lay. Valerie Baxter was a thorn in the side of the force and he didn't want her to become the next easy scapegoat.

When McQueen got back to his office, he started making notes. Within minutes his phone pinged with a message from Tracey Bingham. She had attached the photographs of the footprints with the message, *Size 10 walking boots. Make: Cragtops. Visible identifiable markings on sole.*

McQueen laughed. She was good, very good. He texted back.

Brilliant, Tracey. A brilliant start. She didn't answer.

Twenty-One

McQueen was in his bathroom shaving in the unforgiving glare of the overhead light and thinking, once again, about the twists and turns of his life. A line from an old country and western song drifted through his head, something about was this the life you chose or the one that chose you? He hated country music and didn't know where he'd heard it, but it somehow fitted his mood. He didn't know what had made him so reflective recently, perhaps the frustration of not being able to get close enough to Harper to find out more. It brought back memories of the Marion Connolly case. There was the unavoidable and shockingly harsh reminder of his own mortality caused by finding the lifeless mess of Bainbridge. Death, it was always on the train heading towards you. All you could hope for was a strike at the station or a major derailment to keep the train away from reaching you for a few more years.

What if the grizzled old farmer had really killed himself? McQueen didn't believe it, but was it possible the mysterious chemicals that ebb and flow through the capillaries and cells of our brain tissue had changed him enough to make that happen? Could it be that Bainbridge had suddenly felt hopelessness and depression engulf him? The killer depression, it was a disease like any other. One of the first lectures on depression McQueen had ever attended whilst still an undergraduate, had made a strong impression on him. The lecturer had said telling depressed people to pull themselves together and cheer up was like telling a type-one diabetic to make more insulin in their pancreas. If Bainbridge had been seized by depression, it was entirely possible that the black dog of despair had forced the gun into his mouth.

McQueen put down his razor and stared hard at his reflection. The bruising around his shoulder had almost faded, and his eye was drawn as ever to the physical evidence of the second reason he had chosen to divert the course of his life to flow away from lecturing. It was a livid lumpy line that ran about fifteen centimetres down the centre of his chest.

They'd said that after the open-heart surgery there was a strong chance he'd be depressed. It was something they saw in a lot of patients, they'd said. But for him that hadn't happened. Instead, he'd been so glad to be alive that it had cemented his desire to change the way he lived his life.

He'd been waiting to go down to the operating theatre, and the sombre, handsome, shiny-headed assistant surgeon had come with the consent form for him to sign. He was a serious guy, no bed-side manner or jocularity, straight to the point, but that's what you want from someone who will soon have his fingers in your chest cavity, reasoned McQueen.

The Murder Option

You want a serious person, someone who's been paying attention all his life in lessons, not messing about at the back of the class. In his strange version of a brutally honest pep-talk, the surgeon had made it very clear that the two percent mortality rate for the operation was not to be ignored.

'It means that for every one hundred people we send down to theatre, we *expect* two not to come back alive.' It was the word 'expect' that had done it for McQueen, but rather than terrifying him, it had made him laugh. His levity was not what the surgeon had expected or wanted while he was delivering his very serious information.

'I tell all my patients this,' he added, looking McQueen straight in the eye. 'Two percent is a small number, yes, but it is a *real* number.' His eyes crinkled for a second in a semi-reassuring micro-smile. A nothing-to-worry-about-here smile. Nothing much anyway, and then he passed McQueen the clipboard with the consent form and pen attached.

It was all so final and was delivered with such gravity and meaning, but contrary to the vibe, McQueen fully expected to be in the ninety-eight percent, to come back alive after the double by-pass. Fortunately, he'd been right.

McQueen had spent the next eight hours lying on his back, unconscious and oblivious, while the anaesthetic rendered him absent, his heart and lungs taken off-line and machines took over. His chest was sawn open, intricate work was done by highly skilled fingers, and then it was all put back together again.

The next medical word that had made McQueen chuckle once he was back in the land of the living, although still spaced out on morphine, was *physiotherapy*. It brought to mind injured athletes stretching, lifting weights, and running but for him, physiotherapy had begun with learning to cough without ripping open his stitches. A pillow had to be clasped to his chest and he was made to cough loudly so they could see he was able to clear his lungs if he needed to. It was sore, and he dreaded an unscheduled sneeze.

During the six months it had taken him to get back to normal, in fact better than normal, he made up his mind. He hadn't been given this second chance of life to spend it in lecture halls. It was time to break out and do something more meaningful.

At first, Julie had been supportive of his shift in work focus, or at least on the surface humoured him, but once the monthly salary stopped coming and his new direction and business was slow to take off, the novelty wore off fast. She often asked if he'd have more success if he didn't spend so many mornings dragging his hangover out of bed. When he started to miss social engagements because he was too busy during the evenings and late nights, the relationship pressure mounted. Their old circle of friends thought he was mad, and their opinions were painfully noted by his wife. Her support was withdrawn as they say in the banking industry. But as difficult as it was, he enjoyed his new role on the streets, especially when he had some big wins like the tearful reunion for the missing girl he'd tracked down. He knew should it ever come down to a choice between the job or wife, he'd make the decision that he ultimately did.

McQueen rubbed his itching scar on the keloid lump in the middle. There was nothing Harry Potterish or magical about his mark, but it carried some meaning, nevertheless.

The Murder Option

He snapped out of his reverie and pointed an aggressive finger at his reflected features. 'Come on, get your shit together, mate,' he told his face in the mirror. 'You've got a lead. The anonymous tip-off had to be Harper's assistant, the one who booked your meeting with him, and she might have more to tell you, but just don't frighten her off this time.'

Twenty-Two

It was a tough sell. She really didn't want to meet McQueen, and was mortified he had even contacted her again. She knew he would guess who she was, but had hoped he would leave her alone. At first after a curt goodbye she had put the phone down, but McQueen had gently persisted by email, trying to coax her into a dialogue. The angle he took was she must have things that were weighing heavily on her mind. It wasn't fair she should carry that burden and for the sake of poor Colin Baxter, a man she liked, she could help just by giving McQueen some basic background information. It wasn't much to ask, was it? He suggested she wouldn't want to live the rest of her life with an aching regret. Again she said she didn't want to talk to him, and wary of another restraining order, McQueen was about to give up on her thinking that she was a lost cause when suddenly the subtle pressure paid off and she sent a message saying she would meet him. However, the agreement came with some nervous caveats. It couldn't be in a public place where she might be seen, and it had to be after work. Eventually, she had agreed to come to his office after 8pm, so at 9:15 that night, McQueen was sitting with his patience wearing thin, thinking she must have got cold feet and changed her mind. He'd decided he would give her three hours grace to ruminate and agonise, when at 9:30 there was tap at his door.

When Betty came into his room and took a seat, he vaguely remembered her as the woman who had shown him into Harper's office, but he hadn't paid much attention before and he couldn't have picked her out in a line-up. If he had expected a timid woman who would need to be gently led along, he would have been wrong. Years of working for a sharp and powerful boss had left her toughened and brusque, a graduate of the time-is-money school of business.

'I only came because I want the emails to stop,' she said, forcefully. 'I don't want anything on record, and I don't want to ever be bothered with this again. If you persist, Mr McQueen, I will have to take legal action.'

'Okay,' said McQueen, in a friendly tone. 'But you have to understand, Betty, I'm not trying to hound you or your boss. I'm only trying to find the truth for a grieving widow.'

Betty raised her eyebrows.

McQueen decided to dive straight into some specific questions. She was a woman who was clearly used to being efficient and accurate, and so he thought he'd try to appeal to her professional pride.

'How long have you worked at Harper Engineering, Betty?'

'Eleven years.'

'Wow, long time. You must know just about everything that goes on there.' She didn't respond. 'On the day Colin didn't come in to work, was it you who phoned Mrs Baxter?'

'Yes, it was.'

'Was that because you knew something was wrong straight away?'

'No. As Mr Harper was out on business that day we had no senior managers to sign off invoices, so I wanted to find out if Colin would be coming in or if he was sick. Normally if he was sick, his wife would have let us know.'

McQueen paused. As usual he was recording the interview, but he made a note anyway. He wrote, *she uses 'his wife', not Valerie. No love lost?*

'Yes. Now you say Mr Harper was out of the office. On the Wednesday?'

'Yes. He had an appointment.'

'Do you know who the appointment was with?'

'Mr Harper doesn't tell me all of his appointment details. Some he likes to keep to himself. Sometimes he goes off walking in the hills. He's always been a keen walker. He says he needs it to recharge his batteries.'

'He doesn't tell his PA where he's going to be? Not even for emergencies?'

'He tells me the business things. I usually arrange them for him, but there are others that are more personal, I suppose.'

'Personal?' McQueen took a wild guess. 'Do you mean romantic liaisons, perhaps?'

'I couldn't possibly say,' she answered, actually saying more in her non-answer than she realised.

The Murder Option

McQueen wondered if Betty knew anything about the affair between her boss and Valerie Baxter. Chances were she did, but it also followed she would not want to talk about it. But he had to try.

'Do you know of any possible relationship between Mr Harper and Mrs Baxter?'

It was a step too far for the loyalty of the PA. Betty stared at him unflinchingly for a good ten seconds and then stood up.

'This meeting is over,' she said decisively. 'I wish I'd never spoken to you in the first place. All I did was to overhear a stupid meaningless argument between two businessmen, and I should never have tried to read anything into it. It was stupid of me, and I should have kept my big mouth shut.'

'You had to unburden yourself,' said McQueen, clutching at straws and hoping to tease her back in. 'You did nothing wrong, and something good could come of it.'

'As I said, if you don't leave me alone, legal action will be my next step,' she answered. She was leaving, but he took a last shot. He felt like a doorstep journalist shouting questions at a politician as they clamber without listening into a car to be whisked away.

'Can you tell me about the business? How much of a problem would it have actually been if Mr Baxter had gone to a rival?' But it was too late. She didn't say another word before slamming the door behind her.

The silence that follows the reverberations of a violently banged door leaves its own resounding impression on a quiet, vacated room.

'Can you tell me about the fly-tipping charges?' McQueen asked the empty space she had left.

He looked around his tired office and smiled ruefully. It hadn't been the best interview, and he had to wonder if he was losing his touch because his ability to get people to talk was the very essence of the agency. He shook his head. 'The agency,' he said for the silence around him to hear.

It had all started so well. Initially, in the early heady days of freedom when McQueen felt like school was out forever, he had been excited to set up the agency. The mundane chores of choosing an office, buying filing cabinets, and having business cards printed had all been novel treats. He'd been able to see all the annoying little admin tasks he'd had to do as stepping stones to a bright and wonderful new future where his skills were going to be put to proper use. And early signs had been encouraging. Before he'd even unwrapped his office chair, he'd had the visit that had turned out to be his first real case, and because it had been hugely successful it gave him the false belief his new life would always be like that.

Marcia Graham was a partner in the accountancy firm that worked in the offices above him. She'd seen him move in and, on the first day, had come to him because she said she was sure her husband was gaslighting her. She believed he was trying to make her think she was crazy so he could take control of her and her finances as she'd recently come into a reasonable inheritance.

First, McQueen had assessed her claims to see if she was simply suspicious and paranoid. She wasn't and, in fact, she was more clued in than most people he dealt with on a daily basis. She was one of those good-looking, highly intelligent and successful women who was inexplicably married to a shit. It pained him to think that some might have said the same thing about Julie.

Eager to impress his first client, McQueen had thrown everything he could into the case. He had taken all the neatly written records she'd kept of times, dates, and outrageous events and built a profile of Terry, her husband. Next, McQueen had gone on the hunt and found out the loving hubby had an expensive but secret gambling habit. He'd also been able to trace a succession of her husband's mentally-bruised ex-partners who Marcia knew nothing about. By interviewing the women, McQueen was able to establish a clear pattern of Terry's behaviour, and the likely unfavourable outcome to his actions, supported by hard evidence.

McQueen concluded he was probably going to bleed her dry and then move on, but in the worst-case scenario she was going to end up dead like one of his previous partners who had suffered a fatal stroke after discovering her life savings had evaporated.

The police are often reluctant to act in cases of spousal mental abuse given the *he-said, she-said* dynamics of personal relationships and the difficulty of proving anything, but McQueen was able to provide a dossier of cast-iron evidence for Marcia to take to them that proved to be undeniable.

Even with the evidence, it was still a long haul, and Terry had predictably turned very nasty, which Marcia had bravely braced herself for. He'd tried to coerce her to drop all charges, and this was one of the periods when McQueen would get phone calls in the middle of the night and have to offer his support and reassurance. Phone calls from a distraught crying woman that sometimes meant McQueen then had to get up and go out. Understandably, it had not gone down very well with Julie. It had reignited the suspicions she'd held over Marcia, and led to several arguments which resulted in icy mornings over the silent breakfast table. McQueen was stubbornly refusing to apologise for doing his job, but was also unwilling to explain properly to Julie what was going on, leaving her to stew and suffer.

Eventually all the hard work and preparation had paid-off and resulted in a short custodial sentence for Terry. More thrillingly, Marcia was able to finally free herself from him forever. It was McQueen's first win and coincided with a distinct upturn in his alcohol consumption. Some people drink to hide when they are sad but just as many are spurred on to over-indulge by the invincible feeling happiness gives them. None of this helped the atmosphere in the house, however, and Julie by now had taken to cooking and eating alone.

On the day of Terry's conviction, Marcia had bought McQueen an expensive thank-you dinner, and they'd had a bottle of champagne she didn't touch and McQueen drained. The bubbly had been that night's drinking launchpad for him. Since that meal, he and Marcia had little interaction. They'd seen each other in the office hall a few times and exchanged smiles, but it was as if she didn't want to be reminded of the personal embarrassment of her case. Maybe it didn't fit with the professional image she wanted to project. It was either that, or he'd made such an idiot of himself when they were out that she'd been horrified. As he couldn't remember much about the evening, that was entirely possible.

Twenty-Three

Alone in his flat, McQueen was a bottle of red into his relaxation time and the delivered pepperoni pizza was only one slice away from gone. With a guffaw he remembered the diet sheet they had given him when he'd left hospital. He acknowledged to himself his currently ingested major food groups weren't featured anywhere on the healthy lists. The only thing he could claim as being green was the label on the bottle. He felt it was a careful balance between eating the way they wanted him to, which resulted in him hating his life, or spicing up his plate and glass with the things that were going to make living worthwhile. It was a balance which, stupidly, was heavily tipped to the pleasure side at the moment, in fact, health wasn't getting a look in. That was very stupid, given what he'd been through already. The feeling of invincibility most people carry with them in youth had been well and truly shattered by his faltering heart. His heart attack had come unexpectedly, forty-one was young for a *heart event*, as the medics had termed it. He didn't smoke, he hadn't been particularly overweight or unfit and, at the time, he was drinking a lot less than he was now. He was still drinking above the government's recommended intake units, but who listened to them anyway? And while he was a lecturer he'd still used the subsidised college gym on a regular basis. He had targets and personal bests. He had Lycra and a locker key. He felt he had been doing most things right as far as all the relevant internet health advice was concerned. His job was easy because he was in a well-rehearsed routine and he had a smooth yearly groove. The only stress he'd experienced had been the death of Marion Connolly, but he felt he'd got over that. There was the nagging feeling he could be doing something better with his career, but that was hardly stress. He wasn't fighting fires or saving lives.

He had everything comfortably under control, but what he couldn't control was his genetics, his good old bad genes, the same ones that had seen an end to his father. Maybe it wasn't the death on toast and roll-ups that had got him in the end.

That morning, he hadn't been engaged in a raging argument with Julie or suffered an emotional outburst when the unignorable pain struck. He'd been asleep. It felt like very bad wind squeezing his ribs, but when he cried out, Julie had put the light on to see what the matter was and seen the awful colour of his face. He tried to say he was fine and that it would pass, but she was already calling 999.

He'd drifted into unconsciousness as she pushed hard on his chest having recently done a first-aid course at work. She kept pounding for nine minutes until the paramedics arrived and he owed her his life. It was a heavy debt. Perhaps too heavy in the end. True, she had broken two of his ribs, but as she was fond of saying herself, 'You can take the girl out of Glasgow…'

The cardiologist later explained with alarming cheerfulness that statistically most heart attacks happen in the early hours of the morning when the heart was waking from its slumber. Blood pressure was rising, blood platelets were stickier, and adrenaline was being released. As much as he liked to think of himself as a unique individual, at the end of the day, McQueen had been just another stat on a spreadsheet. He was a mathematical trend, a point on a typical graph.

It was not McQueen's intention, having survived a heart scare, to now join the desperate legions of people who are problem drinkers, but damn it, he wanted another drink. Up to the point of his heart attack he'd lived a fairly clean life, but where had it got him? How much worse could it be if he stopped following the usual health rules?

He'd even printed off and pinned up in his kitchen a quote by the eighteenth-century poet, Alexander Pope:

What some call health, if purchased by perpetual anxiety about diet, isn't much better than a tedious disease.

Life was for living, right? And wine was a blessing sent by the Gods.

He weaved through to the kitchen to open another bottle and raised his glass to one of the stated warning signs of problem drinking — drinking alone. They were slipping down easily. There was a time when this much wine would have sent him straight to sleep, but his resistance was improving, and his liver wasn't perished enough yet to let him down.

The common misconception about alcoholics is that they build up a huge tolerance to alcohol, but McQueen knew from the studies that when someone has destroyed their liver, there is nothing to slow down or take the toxins out of the blood, so the alcohol goes very quickly straight to the brain. McQueen had met winos who could get drunk on one small bottle of stolen aftershave. He wasn't anywhere near that stage yet.

Drink helped him. Yes, he wanted to solve the Baxter case, but in equal measure he wanted to forget all about it. The constant weight of it was getting too painful. He was spending every waking moment juggling with what he knew and thinking of strategies to unlock the door to the truth. He had so little to go on, and even his dreams had become dark visions of dead-ends.

'Fly-tippers', he said. He needed to track them down and see if they could tell him about Harper. Maybe they had been asked to dump the body. Maybe lots of things. His first instinct was to ring Tracey Bingham and ask her to tell him where to find them but fortunately he thought better of it. He'd made the mistake of drunken texts and calls before and learned his lesson. It was very late, and he was too disorientated by alcohol to maintain a clear line of thought or conversation.

He realised he didn't need Tracey, anyway. He could look up the press reports on the internet to see if there were any stories about the dumping incidents. Hadn't Bainbridge

The Murder Option

said some sub-contractors had been charged? All court proceedings make a digital mark, and he had access to some useful databases. He went back to the living room, bottle in hand and opened his laptop, but it was no good, his fingers weren't behaving. He'd have to leave it until the morning. He filled his glass, but he'd dropped off to sleep before he'd had a chance to drain it again.

Twenty-Four

The next morning was a bad one for McQueen. As soon as he opened his eyes he knew he would have to write the day off. Illness that sneaks up and pounces on you while you try to live your life is bad enough, but sickness you seek out and subject yourself to comes with a whole binbag-full of guilt and shame.

It was at times like these he thought of Julie and how attentive and sympathetic she'd been to his hangovers when they had been students together. She'd often been suffering too, and it was yet another thing they shared. Shared guilt is a little easier to bear, but she'd managed to leave student binges back where they belonged, and it wasn't long after that, that the sympathy was replaced by escalating tuts, head shakes, and resentment. At least he didn't have to deal with any of that anymore.

Somehow he had found his way up to bed, but he couldn't remember doing it. With his head anchored deeply in his pillow he found it hard to lift it enough to get up and was only forced to surface by his need for the toilet. Idiot, he told himself, self-absorbed, self-destructive, childish idiot. His self-induced incapacity made a mockery of his high-minded life-affirming stance that having been given another chance at life, he was doing something more productive with it. He went back to bed and slept fitfully for the next three hours ticking off another box on the problem drinker's checklist – work days lost to alcohol. The mashed-up images that assailed him were of Harper, Valerie, Anne, Michael, and Baxter, the latter frozen and grinning as he was, in the framed photo. It was a mixed-up jumble of distorted memories, all with an underlying sense of dread and helplessness.

The physical and mental feelings painfully running through him catapulted his memory back to the incident that had finally seen Julie lose all faith in him; he squirmed when he thought of it now. Through the university, McQueen had been invited to appear on a T.V. show about famous serial killers. He was to be one of the talking heads who added valuable insight like, "he had a taste for killing now and he couldn't stop". The show was a pretty big deal and the opportunities it might have opened up for him would have been enormous. Once he'd become a recognised face and a media-friendly voice of criminology, there would have been a never-ending number of trashy shows to inject a little splash of gravitas into their lurid coverage by a featured academic like him. It could have led to books, speaking slots, and a whole new social circle. Julie had been looking forward to the benefits of fame such as the added kudos they would enjoy amongst their friends and also to being invited to the media parties. She was already counting and spending the extra income it would generate.

On the day of the filming, on the way to the studio, McQueen happened to bump into an old college friend at the train station and they went for a quick lunchtime drink. The quick drink had turned into an all-day and all-night session. He'd missed the recording, and by not even calling the studio to warn them he was not going to make it, had very expensively ruined an afternoon's filming. The production company was not best pleased, and he'd been struck off the list of go-to academic opinions for hire. Julie had never really forgiven him for it, and the crushing shame he'd felt at his apparent helplessness in the face of alcohol had left him bereft for days, at least until he felt well enough to stomach another drink. Things hadn't changed much over time, and he seemed to have learned nothing from the numerous humiliations he'd brought upon himself.

When McQueen finally started to shuffle slowly round his kitchen at 3pm, it was as bad as his first day on his feet after heart surgery. He attempted some dry toast and tea, but his stomach wasn't quite ready for them. And then, like an unwelcome alarm call, the solid impenetrable wall of the Baxter murder loomed in front of him again. His thinking was scattered and muddy and the train of logical progression was lost. He knew he'd had an idea the night before but he couldn't remember what it was. He needed his notes but couldn't see them so he picked up the digital recorder that was lying on the worktop to see if it held any clues. He was surprised to see a voice had recently activated it and even more surprised when he heard the voice was his own. A distorted drunken shout of "Fly-tippers" came back to him and, shaking his head, he hoped he hadn't rung or messaged anyone else while he was in that state.

He knew that a couple of mouthfuls of red might help to settle his mind, but morning drinking was a rickety bridge he hadn't crossed yet. It was another reason why he told himself he wasn't actually an alcoholic because it would be the last and decisive box on the brutal checklist.

He filled a glass with cold tap water instead and forced himself to swallow it, although the effect on his stomach was dreadful. There and then he realised it was no good. The alcohol had to stop. This case was going to be hard enough to get through if he was firing on all cylinders let alone if he was pickling his brain cells at the same time.

'That's it,' he said to the wall that had never once judged or criticised him. 'The next drink I have will be champagne, after I trap this murderer. If I don't get the killer, I will never drink again.' He'd made declarations like this one before, but this time it was different. They always said in the literature that you had to hit rock bottom, but he was nowhere near. McQueen hadn't been soiling the bed or waking up in the street. He hadn't lost all his money, although he no longer had a wife. He hadn't tried to commit suicide or put himself in terrible danger. If he was an alcoholic, he was as high-functioning as it was possible to be, but maybe that was part of the issue. He'd read enough of the literature but wasn't even sure if he was an alcoholic at all. He only knew he'd had enough of being blurred at the edges. He was tired of it, and was tired of himself. He wasn't the stereotype in an alley with a bottle of meths, but he did have a problem, and it was not going away on its own. He was going to change, but this time there was a difference. There was no health professional or nagging wife suggesting, warning, or openly ordering him to do anything. This time he'd decided to get a grip for himself. 'Let's do this,' he said aloud. 'Let's stop drinking, find Colin's killer, and start living this second chance at life the way it deserves to be lived.'

He slumped a little as a queasy wave of nausea rolled through his stomach, but his resolve remained. He was going to give it a go anyway.

Twenty-Five

'It's about my partner, Lia,' blurted out Danny, looking very uncomfortable in his chair.

He had come into the office ostensibly to talk about the McQueen Agency website which he had designed and built a few years before, and had been maintaining ever since for a small monthly fee. Most of McQueen's new clients came through the internet these days, and if nothing else, new punters liked to check out who they were dealing with online before making the scary first phone call. Even more so before the terrifying first visit to the office. McQueen's site went heavy on his academic background, and his perceived differentiator that he wasn't an ex-policeman, which had obviously been the thing which hooked Valerie Baxter. She wasn't the only one, either. There had been a number of prospects who, for various reasons, didn't like the idea their shady business might leak back the police. They weren't necessarily the clients McQueen wanted, straying, as they did, so close to the legal limits of what was acceptable, but he wasn't always in the position to be choosy, and business was business.

Danny had rung down from the Bantaz offices upstairs and said he wanted to pop down to discuss the search engine optimisation on McQueen's site. McQueen was slightly surprised because normally he left all technical decisions to Danny. In fact, it was what he was paid for, not to be dragged into discussions he didn't care or want to care about. But this time Danny was insistent. Apparently putting some different words into the text would boost the site up the search engine rankings to make it easier for new clients to find him. He said he also wanted to talk about the performance of the new automated contact form he'd implemented a few weeks earlier. Newly invigorated as McQueen was, it really wasn't a conversation he wanted to have, but he knew he was paying well under the going rate for the work that Danny did for him, so he figured he'd better at least show some interest.

After a few minutes in the hot seat it was clear Danny had something more personal than digital rankings on his mind. A typically introverted techy and not a natural communicator he hesitated and stumbled even more than usual before he finally got to his point.

Having spent so much time on the site, he was well aware of the services the agency offered, and he'd picked up on McQueen's least favourite, the infidelity investigations.

'Me and Lia have been together for about four years and we've got a two-year-old daughter,' he faltered on. 'But I think Lia might be seeing someone else.' There was a sense of deep pain in his eyes, but none of the white-hot anger

The Murder Option

McQueen usually saw in these circumstances.

'Okay,' he said, managing not to let his weariness show in his tone. 'And why do you think that, Danny?'

'Well, the other day,' he said, 'she was driving. I was in the passenger seat, and we were on our way to her mum's house. And she gets a text from her mum, so she asked me to answer it using her phone, to let them know we were on the way. She unlocked the phone with her thumb, and I started to answer the text and when I was doing it, I couldn't help noticing that her most frequently used emojis were the hearts and kisses.'

'Right,' said McQueen, wondering what he was missing here.

'Don't you see? I'm her partner and she has never, ever sent those to me. So it started me wondering who she was sending them to?'

McQueen recognised the planted seed scenario. It could be the tiniest thing, but once it was buried in the rich soil of male insecurity and jealousy, it grew like a weed.

'I started to scroll through her phone,' continued the clearly distressed young, half-shaven man, in his baggy t-shirt, 'just to see who she'd been texting lately. But she saw me, and she got quite angry, and told me to stop, so I did. Anyway, since then, I've been noticing lots of things, like how long she spends texting on her phone and she always sits so I can't see who she's talking to.' He stopped and sat looking expectantly at McQueen, who was waiting to hear the rest, but there was no more. 'I know you deal with this kind of thing,' said Danny. 'So I just wondered what you thought.'

McQueen thought Danny was an insecure young man who was letting his imagination run away with him. It was a rich vein of income for private investigators all over the country, but it wasn't a branch McQueen was interested in. What this kid needed was relationship counselling, but that wasn't McQueen's chosen area, either. Looking at the guy sitting there so forlornly, though, he could see his concern was real enough, so he tried to be sympathetic and didn't give him his dismissive opinion.

'Okay,' said McQueen. 'And this is all you've got so far?'

'Yes, but I've also noticed she doesn't want to, you know, have sex as often as we used to. And she gets snappy with me really easily.'

'Danny, I'm going to stop you right there and ask you if you've ever heard of something called confirmation bias?'

'Not sure,' he mumbled, meaning that he hadn't.

'Okay, Google it when you go upstairs. It means the way the human brain works is once you believe something, you start looking for evidence that supports your belief. You can't help ignoring anything that doesn't agree with how you already feel. So I think you shouldn't jump to conclusions. If she was having an affair, she would probably have another phone, and she certainly wouldn't let you touch her phone, not even in the car. The other stuff, that's because you're in a long-term relationship. That's how they go unless you live in an advert.'

He knew he was being a bit short with him, but he really didn't have time for this. He had a real case to solve, and his patience had worn thin. 'Now, if you really want to pay me sixty pounds an hour to follow her around with a camera for

The Murder Option

a few weeks, then be my guest. My bank balance could certainly do with it. Oh, and by the way, if she's as innocent as I think she probably is and finds out you've asked me to do that, then you can say goodbye to the relationship anyway. I think the words *paranoid* and *controlling* might crop up in the argument you'll have.'

'So what are you saying?' asked the would-be client he didn't want.

'On balance, you want my advice? Talk to her. Don't make it an accusation. If you really can't let the emoji thing go, and it's really bugging you that much, then ask her, but in a jokey way, like, "Hey, what's with the heart emojis by the way? You don't send them to me." And then, when she gives you a completely reasonable response like she sends to her mum or something, you forget the whole thing forever.'

Danny was scared.

'But what if it goes the other way? What if she says she's been texting her boss Josh at work for instance, and now I've brought it up she's leaving me?'

'Then that was going to happen, anyway, and you've found out without spending sixty quid an hour.'

'Okay, if that's what you think,' said Danny. He wasn't convinced. 'Thanks. I'll give it a shot and I'll let you know how it goes.'

'Anyway,' said McQueen as Danny's hand was on the door handle. 'What about my website?'

'Oh, it's fine,' answered Danny waving his hand. 'That was just an excuse to come down to talk to you. You leave the optimisation to me, and I won't tell you how to catch murderers.'

'Deal,' said McQueen.

This, he thought, *this is why even a frustrating, muddled, difficult murder case is better than business as usual.*

As soon as he had left, McQueen turned his newly clear-thinking focus to the only lead he still had. Browsing the various online news reports, McQueen found Bainbridge had been correct. A case of fly-tipping had been brought against Harper Engineering two years before, and it was based on photographs the farmer had taken of one of their lorries in the act. Bags of building rubble and various other sacks of industrial waste had been found in the field and some of them were traceable back to Harper's company. It was potentially serious for them, with possible fines running up to fifty grand, and even imprisonment a possibility for repeat offenders. A company spokesperson had made an official statement saying a rogue sub-contractor had acted without any authority and that Harper Engineering knew nothing about it. The spokesperson was named as Colin Baxter. A driver called Shane Daley had eventually been charged but, due to lack of evidence, the charges had been dropped.

What McQueen wanted to know was what Martin Harper's involvement in the crime had really been. Did he even know where the field was, and could he have used it to dump Baxter's body? Clearly, Harper wasn't going to tell him anything. He'd already distanced himself from the whole thing, but the man who'd been made scapegoat might have had a view.

McQueen went to the laptop. He spent a lot of time tracing people. He had access to a number of specialist databases, and finding a man whose name had been in the

The Murder Option

press wasn't too hard. Within five minutes, McQueen had Shane Daley's reported place of employment, and he was on his way there.

Twenty-six

McQueen went into the café, bought a tea, and made his way over to the table where a man in a hi-vis jacket was tucking into a plate of egg, beans, chips, and grease. He was big, possibly thirty years old, and very possibly thirty stone in weight. He was hunched over a small table, and his dirty blond hair was unfashionably long. He looked exactly like the image that had been cruelly described to McQueen by the guy's boss.

'Shane?' asked McQueen. The man didn't even look up, he just nodded, and McQueen took that as an invitation to sit down. 'Your foreman said I'd find you in here.'

'Congratulations. You did it. You found me,' said Shane sarcastically, looking at him for the first time.

'My name's McQueen, and I just wanted to ask you a couple of questions. Is that okay?'

'Are you the police?'

'No, I'm a private investigator, and I'm making some inquiries.'

'A private dick,' said Shane nastily. 'How exotic.' Shane

The Murder Option

hadn't stopped eating. He seemed to be in some kind of race, as if on a food challenge to cram as many calories into his face as possible in the shortest amount of time.

'Listen, Shane, as I say, I'm not from the police, and I've got no interest in you, but I know you got stuck with a fly-tipping charge a while ago. Dumping rubble in a field, wasn't it? I know you were just the truck driver, but it sounds like you ended up taking the heat. Seems a bit like you took a hit for someone else on that one.' The big man carried on chewing, but he held up his wrist to show his watch.

'Strict dinner hour,' he said through a mouthful of chips. 'I've got fifteen minutes left, so get to the point, your majesty.' *Your majesty*. McQueen hadn't heard that joke since school.

'It's not about the fly-tipping, that's long gone, but—'

'And all charges were dropped,' butted in Shane, pointing his knife which was dripping with ketchup at him.

'Absolutely. You're an innocent man, but like I say, I'm not interested in you. I'm interested in Martin Harper, the owner of Harper Engineering. I'm trying to find out how much Martin Harper himself had to do with that trip. Was it his idea to use that field?'

Shane shovelled the last forkful into his mouth and then clattered his cutlery down onto his plate. He reached for his mug of coffee and appraised McQueen carefully.

'Fifty quid and I'll tell you as much as you want to know,' he said. McQueen smiled. It was all about economics in the end, and in Shane's world you had to take your breaks where you found them.

'Let's say twenty quid, but only if the information is any good.'

'Let's see it.' McQueen dug in his wallet and pulled out a twenty which he put on the table, then rested his elbow on.

'So, Harper?' he asked again.

Shane sat back, his bulk dwarfing the chair beneath him. 'You're an investigator, right? Well, ask yourself this. What would a big company like Harper Engineering be doing messing about with fly-tipping? These days, for big companies, it's all about recycling and meeting waste targets. Think about their reputation. Why would they risk it? Fly-tipping is for small-time builders who don't want to pay for permits or cowboy site clearance outfits. Check for yourself. Harper has a professional waste management company. They don't need to dump stuff.'

'Well someone did, and there are photos to prove it, so what are you saying?'

'I'm saying he had nothing to do with it. Harper. Someone else told me where I'd find the lorry and where to get rid of the rubbish. And I think he knew I'd get caught. If you're asking me, I think it was a smear job on the company, to make 'em look bad. I was paid to do one run, and I was paid to keep my mouth shut. They told me it would never get to court and it didn't.' He checked his watch again and reached for the twenty.

'Who?' asked McQueen. 'Who gave you the lorry?'

'I never met him. All done over the internet and the keys and cash were on the seat of the truck when I got there. I put the truck back where I found it and that was supposed to be the end of it.'

The Murder Option

'Would you know how to trace this person if you needed to?'

'Not for twenty quid, I wouldn't,' replied Shane. It all sounded dodgy to McQueen but there was still a chance Shane was telling the truth.

'So, tell me,' said McQueen. 'You seem to know how it all works. Who would I go to if I wanted something else dumped, like a body?'

'I've got no idea,' he said. 'But if you've got one to get rid of, try looking on the internet.' He pulled the twenty from the table before leaving.

McQueen sat and finished his tea. Shane met every criterion of an unreliable witness, a person who was ready to do just about anything for cash and would be shredded in court by a barrister. Every single thing Shane had said could have been a lie, but on gut feeling alone, McQueen believed his story anyway. He felt confident in his ability to spot liars, and Shane didn't succeed in lighting any of the usual warnings. It wasn't good news for the case, though, he hadn't got what he wanted, and now there were a couple of new possibilities adding more mud to the already murky water. Could it be that someone with a grudge against Harper Engineering first tried to ruin their reputation and then murdered the second in command? McQueen had been doing exactly what he said he wouldn't do in blindly chasing Martin Harper when there was always the chance it had nothing to do with him at all. He'd warned Danny about confirmation bias only to be seduced by it himself.

The other possibility was that whoever had paid Shane to dump the rubble had also paid him to dump the body in the same place.

McQueen needed some clarity, a chance to hear his thoughts out loud and argue the points, but as a sounding-board, the walls of his office weren't going to be enough this time. Luckily, he had another option now.

Twenty-seven

Tracey was kicking the ragged and slobber-covered tennis ball across the grass, and the heavy black labrador was happily bringing it back every time, until eventually he got bored and left it in the grass behind them. Tracey went back for the ball, picked it up, and put it, wet with slobber, into a poo-bag before dropping it into her pocket.

'He was brought up with the sea and the sand, so it's been an adjustment for him to get used to grass and ponds. I had to drag him out of that one the other day, he was after a duck. The poor kids who were feeding them were terrified.'

It was her day off and they were sauntering across the north-eastern end of Roundhay park towards the folly, a castle that had never been a castle except in the imagination of kids with bows and arrows. She seemed a lot less business-like in the presence of Charlie, her dog. He had a softening effect. She said she had inherited him when the owner died and then they had both relocated from Cornwall. McQueen asked why she had moved away from the South West, but all she said was that she had outgrown her old life.

'To come so far could almost be seen as running away,' ventured McQueen, but she shook her head.

'Not really, but when people think of you as one thing, it's hard for them to adjust to thinking of you in a new way. I was successful in the job, but some people struggled to accept it, so I decided to transfer for a new start.'

'I know what you mean,' said McQueen. 'I was a university lecturer and jacked it in to do this. Some people never got used to the change, mainly my ex-wife.'

'What was your specialty?'

'Forensic psychology and criminology.'

'Makes sense,' she said. 'I have a degree in sociology and look at me now, questioning Saturday night drunks about fights they've started and the damage they've done. Is that what made her an ex, you changing careers?'

'It was part of it, I think. She moved up here with me from London when I got the position at the uni and then I moved the goalposts.'

'Did she move back?'

'No, she had a job up here by then, so she's still here, in our old house, in fact.'

They chatted easily about their separate experiences of the stark differences between theory and reality for a while and then arriving at an open-air café they sat down at an empty table. Charlie was reluctant to have his lead put on but, as Tracey explained, left to his own devices he would be jumping up at the tables and clearing people's plates of any food he could get near.

Sitting with steaming hot chocolates in front of them, she suddenly changed gear and became more focused. She asked why he'd wanted to meet up and specifically, did he have any news for her regarding an arrest? He opened the creased notebook he had brought with him. In the emptiness of his living room, without even the crutch of alcohol, he had decided he had to trust her. He had no choice really; the investigation was going nowhere. So many crimes these days were solved by laboratory science, DNA, and microscopic hairs. They had none of that. They were blind. All they had were photographs of some boot prints which may or may not have something to do with the case. They also had the driving force of the suspicion of a grieving widow's accusations. He took her through his recent meagre findings, flipping through his book.

He told her about Betty the PA and how it appeared that Harper had no alibi for the day of the murder, but how she was not going to be any kind of witness against her boss. He'd been out on business, but that business might have been personal pleasure, hence his reluctance to talk about it.

'It would be good to know what he says about that,' said McQueen. 'But, of course, as we know there was no official interview of Harper.' Then he told her about Shane Daley and the big man's ideas about what the fly-tipping episode was about, but how he believed Harper had nothing to do with any of it. Tracey listened to his latest hypothesis about someone with a grudge trying to ruin Harper Engineering. She made no comment.

'There are a couple of important things we need to know, Tracey,' he said. 'But it's not going to be comfortable for you. We need to eliminate Harper as a suspect, but to do that we need to know what Harper says he was doing that day. I've heard there was an off-the-record interview, which brings us to the other major piece of missing information. Why do the police seem to be protecting him?'

He looked at Tracey. She didn't seem to be outraged. She sipped from her cardboard cup and nodded.

'You're right,' she answered. 'And I've already tried to get that information and got nowhere. I'm the newbie in town. I've already had a visit from the two uniformed officers who came to see you at your house. They were very keen that I stop associating with you and made it clear it wouldn't do my reputation any good around the station. And DS Brooks, the man who took your witness statement after the death of Bainbridge, said something similar. So you see, I've made myself unpopular and I have to be careful how I tread.'

'Is it getting too hot for you?' asked McQueen, genuinely concerned for her mental welfare.

'I've been in hotter places,' she answered, unfazed. 'But it sounds like I'm going to have to try a bit harder if I'm going to find anything out.'

There was something else McQueen wanted to say and it had also been born of a sober night of reflection. He'd tried to look honestly at his professional weaknesses to see where he could improve. There was no point taking a new life path unless it was going to be successful. The world didn't need another half-assed private investigator. The thing that was going to satisfy his need to contribute to society in some meaningful way, was whether he could take on the right cases and produce more results for his clients. Now that Tracey had mentioned her present discomfort in her role, it seemed like a perfect time to bring it up.

'Listen,' he said. 'I know you have your career and I

know you're going to be very good at what you do in the future and you could really climb the heights, but regardless of this case, if it doesn't work out for you, I want you to consider joining me.'

'What as?'

'A partner, of course. A business partner and investigator, that is. Your name on the door next to mine?' He saw confusion cross her face. 'I know you don't need it right now,' he added quickly, 'but please bear it in mind.'

She didn't laugh, which had been a reaction he would have understood, instead she said, 'This is kind of sudden, isn't it? I mean, Mr McQueen, I hardly know you.' And then more seriously, in case he was getting the wrong idea she said, 'you understand I'm not looking for any kind of personal relationship, don't you?'

'Me neither,' assured McQueen.

'Yes, but just to get this crystal clear,' said Tracey, looking straight at him. 'I'm not looking for a relationship at the moment, but when I do find a partner, she'll be younger and prettier than you.'

McQueen smiled. 'Fair enough. I understand, but I only ever intended this to be completely professional,' assured McQueen. 'I've already seen you have some important skills I'm lacking and, above all, I need this.' He waved his hand vaguely to indicate the meeting they were currently having. 'I need to have someone who understands the game, someone analytical to discuss these cases with, someone with police experience. It's too easy for me to get bogged down in my own obsessions.'

'Well,' she said, taking hold of Charlie's lead to pull him

to his feet. 'Thanks for the offer, McQueen, and I will give it some thought, but for now I'm very happy to be a working copper. My career has only just started, and as you can probably imagine in the macho culture of policing, I face a few more credibility challenges than most. But I don't give up easily. If it wasn't difficult, it wouldn't be worth doing.'

'Think of it as a safety net,' he said, also standing up. 'If the frustrations prove too much and things don't work out in the force. A not very safe and not very comfortable safety net.'

Twenty-eight

It was time for McQueen to get his house in order. He'd gone into the office very early and started on the paperwork. It was one of the benefits he'd found in not drinking, it had given him back those many hours in the morning that, in the past, he'd had to spend nursing his aching body and fuzzy head. He worked through the spreadsheets, sent out some invoice reminders, printed off some client case reports, and answered all his emails. He ignored lunch and, by mid-afternoon, was feeling the satisfaction of some pressure released.

His plan was to clear the decks and then, with a fresh focus, renew his efforts in finding Colin Baxter's killer. He wanted to give Valerie an update but wanted to have something positive to say when he did. He wanted no distractions nagging at the back of his mind. That was the plan.

On his desk his phone vibrated, and he looked at the name that had come up on the screen. He sighed and shook his head. Wasn't it Woody Allen who'd said, "if you want to make God laugh, tell him about your plans."? It was actually his version of the old Jewish proverb, *man plans, and God laughs,* but the truth in the saying was unavoidable, as soon as McQueen had ever made a plan in his life, something had come along to derail it.

He looked at his flashing phone screen. There was one job McQueen couldn't ignore, not even for a murder case, and this was it. It had come to him through a referral a couple of years before from Angus, his accountant, and it alone kept him financially afloat. More than that, though, it had almost become a personal obligation, a promise to keep someone safe.

Knowing McQueen was struggling, Angus had passed him on a very rich client who had one recurring job for which McQueen was on a decent retainer. The money paid the rent on the office and most of his living expenses and, without it, he'd have sunk long ago. For that he was grateful, but it was not a job he enjoyed.

The client was a very rich older woman called Grace whose twenty-five-year-old errant grandson had lived with her in her beautiful townhouse ever since he'd been disowned by his despairing parents. Unfortunately for Grandma, Tom, the grandson, was a recovering drug addict and from time to time would have spectacular relapses. He'd take a bunch of cash from a drawer and go missing for weeks into the lost lands of Leeds. She would be beside herself with worry once she discovered he'd gone again and then she'd ring McQueen.

She never cared about the missing money, but on a semi-regular basis McQueen would be tasked with tracking Tom down, bringing him back, seeing that he went back to rehab and restoring the calm. One of the reasons the old lady had employed McQueen was she thought his psychological background might help keep Tom on the straight and narrow, but she was wrong. Addiction was not a strong point with McQueen.

In their first ever meeting, Grace had quizzed him at length about what he did. He was used to the client pitch and said he'd originally trained as a forensic psychologist and criminologist. Then when she hadn't quite understood, he'd had to say that no, he wasn't a psychiatrist. Like a lot of people, she'd imagined the word forensic was only attached to the people she saw on the news in blue coveralls who were gathering blood and fingerprints after a crime. He'd explained it just meant the appliance of science to crime, and *his* science was psychology. In the end she'd decided that, despite what he'd said and the patience of his explanation, he was after all some kind of psychiatrist and the right man to find and look after her darling Tom.

Still, as a job after the first time it was never that difficult to find Tom again. He had the same haunts and the same junkie friends, and no one is readier to give you information for money than a junkie. McQueen had set up a little network of trusted informants so anytime Tom showed up, his so-called friends knew where they could cash in the tip-off. Naturally, it was cash McQueen charged back as expenses. McQueen would then show up at the disgusting flat or tent and coax Tom back to the patient non-judgmental love of his grandma. Tom never gave McQueen any trouble, it was as if the binge was his little well-earned holiday and he was reluctant but ready to go home. McQueen had grown to like Tom. He was posh and polite and could be quite charming, but he was glad he wasn't a son of his and could understand how it had all become too painful for his parents.

McQueen answered the phone. The old woman was crying and distraught and his heart went out to her. She really cared for the boy and yet he could still put her through this. He'd been gone for two days now and she had discovered some of her jewellery was missing.

'There was no money, you see. I had no money in the house.' She seemed to be apologising for not having left money around for him to steal. Bizarrely, it reminded McQueen of something Julie had once said when they returned home to a burgled flat. Surveying the devastation, she'd said she'd have preferred to have left the equivalent cash inside the front door with the message, "take the money, but don't trash the flat."

'Don't worry,' said McQueen reassuringly. 'I'll make some calls and find him for you. He'll be fine.'

'Oh, will you?' she asked in her shaking but still cut-glass accent. 'That would be so kind if you could.' McQueen could see where Tom got his politeness in times of stress from.

What he never said to her was that there was the very real chance he wasn't fine, of course, that he was lying somewhere overdosed and glassy-eyed, with vomit on his face and stuck in his throat. Ugly death was always McQueen's main concern when he got the call, not because it would mean an end to his regular income, but that Grace would not be able to cope with the news.

After giving her a few more calming assurances, McQueen put the phone down. He closed the Baxter

The Murder Option

notebook. He needed a break anyway and Baxter wasn't going anywhere. The sooner he found Tom the more likely it was that he would still be alive, and a breathing person was always going to take precedence over a dead one.

Twenty-nine

Searching for Tom always forced McQueen way out of his comfort zone, literally out into the uncomfortable areas of outer Leeds he preferred to avoid. Like many cities, the shiny centre of Leeds had seen a lot of investment and regeneration in recent years. Property prices had risen steadily, and trendy bars and cafés had proliferated in the surrounding affluent areas. Something was always being built and something was always changing. McQueen often wondered how long it would be before he was ejected from his offices so developers could move in to make their quick buck. The city had reinvented itself as something of a financial centre, too, and there was the massive PR boost of the relocation of the new Channel 4 headquarters to the city. Things were happening, but there were still a lot of people in Leeds who saw none of it. The trickle-down economy theory had yet to sprinkle its wealth on many of the long-term residents of this Yorkshire jewel. Areas of Leeds were still statistically designated as some of the most deprived in the country based on the uptake of benefits and lack of employment. Crime fighting forces across the globe knew the devastating equations in play. Where there was conspicuous wealth, there was usually a requirement for trendy drugs like cocaine and where there was poverty, there was a demand for anything they could get their hands on.

Three miles south of McQueen's flat were the various council estates of the romantically named Belle Isle suburban catchment. It was as good a starting point for his search as any. Driving in, McQueen always wondered how many hapless French tourists might have wondered in looking for their beautiful island. The only island they would have found was a large, open green circle of land right in the centre, Belle Isle Circus, that had once been a tram terminal and was now a roundabout green space. Surrounded by dull, regimented, red-brick semi-detached council properties, it was the kind of place that could actually look quite pleasant on a sunny day and drain your soul on a bleak winter's evening. It was true that plenty of perfectly happy people made their lives here, contented families surrounded by relatives and friends making the best of what they had. But there were also the places which saw the sharp end of what a community living with poverty produces. Emergency services' sirens were a common audio backdrop.

First McQueen went to a particularly messy-looking council house whose occupants had about the same regard for gardening as he did. Generally, McQueen wasn't one for decorating his front garden with brightly coloured, broken, plastic toddler-toys. It was where he'd found Tom the last time he had disappeared. He didn't expect him to be there and he wasn't, but with a little financial oiling he got another address to check from the current inhabitants. *Is there anyone looking for you two?* he wondered as he left the two young men to their spaced-out afternoon.

After a couple more personal visits and the feeling that perhaps he was just being given the runaround, he arrived at a basement flat in Morley and was let in by a woman who bore all the tell-tale physical signs of an addict. Skin, teeth, hair, and eyes all advertised the poisons her blood and soul couldn't do without. It was the part of this job of tracking down Tom he hated most, having to confront the elements of society he, and most other people, would rather forget about.

'Is Tom here?' he asked.

She turned and went back inside leaving the door open. He felt desperately sorry for her, not that his pity helped her much. *Once you were very a pretty daughter*, he thought, *before the drugs attacked you.* Inside he was dreading seeing the obligatory child in nappies toddling through the squalor, but she led him down the narrow corridor and pointed inside the front room. The curtains were shut, but in the gloom, McQueen could make out the usual detritus of drug abuse paraphernalia lying everywhere. The things to avoid were any discarded needles that might be sticking up like disease carrying porcupines waiting for a careless foot. There were two men slumped on a sofa watching the space where a TV must have once been before it was stolen or sold. Thankfully, one of the men was Tom, and as he slowly looked up, McQueen saw recognition flicker in his eyes.

'Ah,' he said with a grin. 'My fairy godmother. Grandma's little helper come to rescue me from the clutches of evil.'

McQueen was feeling relieved he'd found his quarry,

The Murder Option

alive but not necessarily well.

'There's someone very worried about you, Tom, and I think we should go and see her. Come on.' He put out his hand to help him up but the other man next to Tom on the sofa suddenly stirred.

'Wait a minute, hold on, hold on, maybe he doesn't want to go. Maybe you are taking him against his will and he's a grown man. He can make his own decisions and if he doesn't want to go he doesn't have to.' He was a wiry little guy with a dirty splodge of an indistinguishable blue tattoo on his neck and the aggressive tone of a man very used to arguments. He looked like prison to McQueen. McQueen knew exactly what was going on. The junkie had found a cash-cow in the shape of Tom and was probably hopeful that the posh guy's money would keep on coming. McQueen was in no mood for this, but he knew any sign of reasonable negotiation would be seen as weakness.

'I advise you to shut up,' he said, standing over the man. 'But if you want to report a kidnapping, I can call the police right now and get them down here.' He took his phone from his pocket. 'I'm sure they'd like an excuse to be invited in to look around and see what they might find.'

The man's demeanour changed instantly. 'Calm down, buddy. No need for all that,' he said with what he must have thought passed as a charming smile. It might have been if it hadn't been for the missing teeth.

'By the way,' said McQueen. 'Where's the jewellery?'

The guy held up both hands to show they were empty. 'No idea what you're talking about,' he said, still toothlessly grinning. McQueen was aware anything Tom had taken from his grandmother's house had already been converted into drugs and was in their veins by now, but he wanted the man to know this could go further if it needed to.

'Everything cool, Billy?' asked a female voice behind him, and McQueen turned to see the same woman who had let him in standing at the door with a samurai sword in her hands. He still felt sorry for her. This was her life. It included days when she had to go and get a weapon to protect her man. She didn't look like she was going to attack him. In truth, she didn't look as if she was capable but looks could be deceptive.

'It's okay, babe,' said Billy from the couch. 'Tom's going with his mate. But he'll be back. Don't worry about that.'

McQueen pulled Tom to his feet and they eased out of the room past the woman and her blade, now lowered. 'See you later, mate,' shouted Billy.

'Yeah,' said Tom.

When they were in the car, McQueen mulled over all the things he'd said before to this young man sitting next to him and how none of it ever made any difference. Although he really wanted to, it was no good telling him what he was doing to his grandmother. He'd said all that already and nothing had changed. Tom had been through rehab a number of times so knew all the recovery points. He'd heard he should be avoiding triggers and keeping away from his old friends. He'd been told routine was important and that support was there if he needed it. But the other thing to know was that relapses happen and life wasn't hopeless.

'I didn't like your friend, Billy, much,' said McQueen, starting the car.

The Murder Option

'Ah, he's okay,' answered Tom. 'He's had some bad breaks, but he's alright.'

He knew it was judgemental, but McQueen couldn't help himself.

'He's not okay, Tom. If you were seeing straight you'd know that. You know you're just a source of money to him, don't you?' Tom turned in his seat to look at him.

'Like I am to you?' It was a dart that hit home, but it wasn't the whole truth.

'Yes, I do get paid for bringing you home, Tom, but now I know you, I'd do it for your grandmother anyway.' He left a significant pause and stared straight at the young addict who still had so much ahead of him, all he needed to do was want it. 'I'd do it for you, too, Tom. You're worth more than this.'

McQueen drove him back to the house and they pulled up outside. Tom seemed to have straightened out enough to be taken in without shocking his grandma too much, but McQueen hesitated.

'Would you do me a favour, Tom?' he asked. 'It's quite a big favour, but I need your help.' Tom was looking sceptical, as if there was nothing in the world he could possibly offer. 'I've recently stopped drinking,' continued McQueen. 'I'm not an alcoholic, at least I don't think I am, but the drink was affecting my professional life, actually. If I'm honest it was affecting my whole life, but the main thing is I've got a difficult murder case at the moment that's not going very well, and I need to be clear headed. I've got a young police detective called Tracey to compete with. She's sharp and fast, and I need to keep up and I can't do it at the moment. It's stressful and I can't say giving up has been very easy and it's only been a few days, but would you help me?' Tom looked blankly back at him. 'I mean like a sponsor, someone I can call if I feel the urge to drink coming on.'

'Why me?'

'Because no one knows this shit like you, Tom, that's why. Maybe you can save me before I really need saving.'

They sat silently for a few minutes, before Tom spoke. 'And this isn't just psychology and rehab talk? It's not just you trying to give me responsibility and someone else to think about other than myself?' Tom was an intelligent kid and there was no point trying to fool him. The only thing that was going to make this work was honesty.

'Yes, there is a bit of that, I suppose. Like I said, I know I'm not a full-on addict like you, and I don't want to patronise you, but I do see a problem looming on my horizon. Maybe now is the time to address it before I really do have a dependency. I really think we could help each other.'

'I haven't been much help to anyone else,' he replied. 'But if you want to call me, you're welcome to.' They exchanged numbers and agreed McQueen would check in at least once a week, just to say how it was going.

'You know what they say about alcohol addiction in rehab?' asked Tom, one hand on the door catch. 'They say it's insidious, it creeps up, it spreads like a stain, slowly, slowly taking over. Maybe you're right. Maybe now's the time to act. Maybe that's what I should have done way back when I was naïve enough to think I had it all under control.'

When they eventually went into the house, the old

The Murder Option

woman's relief and joy at seeing her grandson was all the payment McQueen would have needed. Unfortunately, his landlord wouldn't have seen it like that.

As McQueen was about to leave, confident that Tom wasn't about to run straight out of the door, Grace came over to him.

'Thank you,' she said, and then reached out her thin arms to give him a hug. It was something she'd never done before, and McQueen was slightly taken aback. He felt her skinny arms encircle him and she whispered, 'It's never been more important than now that Tom is home. I need him near me.'

'Is there anything else you need from me,' ventured McQueen, sensing something was different.

'No,' she said, pleasantly. 'You've done the best thing possible at the moment already.' Then the old woman moved away to go to speak to Tom. McQueen looked over at the lad and made the thumb and little finger gesture for phone to him and then left the two alone.

Thirty

Charlie the dog was sniffing at a much smaller terrier and wouldn't leave the poor thing alone. No amount of shouting from Tracey was having any effect because he was deafened by animal passion. The terrier's owner, a middle-aged woman in a green quilted jacket, was getting quite irate, so Tracey jogged over with the lead and hauled Charlie away. When she was out of earshot of the woman she said to McQueen, 'If she takes her out when she's in season, what does she expect?'

They had to head in the opposite direction for quite a way before Tracey felt confident enough to take Charlie's lead off again. They had been chatting about nothing during the walk, but it was Tracey who had called, so McQueen was waiting to hear her update.

'It's not been easy,' she said. 'A police station is usually a rumour mill just like anywhere else, but there's a closed shop when they don't trust you yet. Everyone is wary of a spy in the camp, I suppose.'

'No luck then?' he asked.

'Some luck,' she answered, with a little smile. 'The key was in the powerful camaraderie of team sports.' McQueen

The Murder Option

looked quizzically at her. 'Basically I've joined the station volleyball team, and I've become friendly with one of the other women. We had a few drinks last night after practise.' She stopped walking to pick up a stick and throw it for Charlie. 'But before I go any further, first, let me lay out the ground rules so there can be zero confusion. One thing you must understand is that anything I say to you must not make it to your friends in the press. Ever. If it does, then I'll know it came from you, and we're done.'

'You can trust me,' he said. 'For one thing, me and the press aren't so friendly any more, not since they hung me out to dry. And secondly, with you I'm looking at a future professional partnership, not a short-term hit.'

'Alright, well, it's only rumour. It's gossip of the worst kind, and I don't know if it's true, but it would make sense.'

'Okay,' said McQueen. 'Understood.'

'It turns out that Martin Harper is a bit of a local big-shot, big local employer and supports a few charities. He's into all that roundtable and mason's club nonsense, so he gets invited to a lot of social functions. He mingles with the great and the good, and one of those just happens to be a Chief Constable.'

'Right, so he's the one protecting Harper?'

'Not exactly. The very nasty rumour has it that at one of these black-tie dinners, Martin Harper was sitting next to the chief constable's wife. They hit it off, and you can guess the rest.'

'Ah, ladies' man. That kind of fits with his relationship with Valerie Baxter, the wife of another one of his friends. I must say, it sounds a bit risky to be seeing a chief constable's wife, but maybe it added to the thrill for him.'

'Yes, but here's the bit you don't want to hear. The word is that on the morning of the murder that's exactly where he was, in the arms of the chief constable's wife.'

'Christ, so that's why he wanted to keep it on the quiet?'

'Exactly. He wasn't protecting him, he was protecting her. If Harper had to give an official statement with his alibi, then her name gets dragged into it, and it's humiliation all round.'

'And do you believe these rumours?'

'Based on who told me, yes I do, and it would explain a lot. They aren't covering up for a murderer which would be a huge step for the police. They know he didn't do it. But they don't want to go into details about *how* they know.'

McQueen mulled it over as they sauntered back to the cars. It seemed like Harper was well and truly out of the picture which put McQueen back to square one. He'd have to speak to Valerie Baxter. If she knew there was no chance he was going to be bringing Harper in, then she might want to stop his investigation, or at least stop paying for it. He'd warned her she might not get the result she wanted, but she'd been so sure of her ground he wasn't sure she had listened.

Thirty-one

McQueen laid all his notes out on the desk and started listening again to the recordings he'd made, this time with the viewpoint that, although Martin Harper might register highly on the psychopathic index, and in fact promiscuity and risk taking were yet more tell-tale traits, he couldn't be the murderer. The best lead he had now was the fly-tipping angle and whoever had paid Shane Daley to implicate Harper Engineering.

He'd rung Valerie and told her Harper had a cast-iron alibi, and that although he couldn't share it with her, it wasn't going away. She'd have to accept Harper wasn't the one. He told her about the fly-tipping and how he wanted to pursue that. If he could find out who had it in for Harper Engineering then he might be able to find out who the killer was. She listened carefully as he reiterated his quest had always been about justice for Colin, and that was still ongoing, but he understood she might have lost faith in him. She was very quiet and said she would have to think about what she wanted to do next.

It was all getting tough, and he felt one glass of wine

would make everything a bit easier, free-up the thought processes, and maybe inspire some insight. But he recognised the destructive pattern that was forming in his mind. It was the self-justifying path to painful excess, so he put a call in to Tom instead. He sounded relaxed and healthy, and they talked for an hour about the benefits of being sober. He treated Tom as the expert who then rose to the expectation. There was nothing really ground-breaking said by either of them, but when the call was over, McQueen felt better and his need for a drink had receded. It was weird, as if he didn't want to let Tom down. Tom had been letting other people down for years. But that wasn't the point, he was trying to lead by example.

He remembered Valerie's quiet response to his phone call and it brought to mind her room stuffed with furniture, and he remembered the sideboard she'd pointed at. It occurred to him he had dismissed it at the time but perhaps it was time to sit and go through the sympathy cards Valerie had received after Colin's death. Could it be that the murderer would have sent a card? It was a sick idea, but what was sicker than sticking a knife into someone? The task would at least give McQueen a list of people who knew Colin. It could be a mammoth task to follow all those up, a task much more suited to a well-resourced police force, but he was clutching at straws now and nothing was a bad idea.

An hour later, just as McQueen was about to go home, he received an email that made it clear he wasn't going to be getting any further Baxter cooperation and that sifting through the personal correspondence was going to be out of the question:

The Murder Option

Dear Mr McQueen,

Thank you for your time, but I shall no longer require your services. My brother and I agree that if you will not continue to gather evidence to convict Martin Harper, we shall have to find someone else who will.

Please drop off with me all the notes and evidence you have accumulated so I can pass them on. Everything. I have paid you for this investigation and I no longer want you to work on this case at all so you will not need them.

Thank you, Valerie Baxter

McQueen sighed. It was a shame she felt like that, but it was her choice. She sounded quite adamant about his records but she certainly wasn't going to get her hands on his notes and recordings. He would prepare a final report and invoice as he always did and let her have those but cooperation or not he wasn't finished with this case even if she was finished with him.

164

Thirty-two

He was on the edge of sleep when some vague mixture of images and memories swirling in his unconscious coalesced to form a red-hot poker that stabbed right through his dreaminess and woke him. Eyes open, McQueen sat upright, his rapid breathing was matching his racing heartbeat. His hand moved automatically to scratch his itching chest scar. For a second, he thought he'd heard a noise, but then it came back to him, the revelation that had cut through his slumber. Something he remembered, something had been there all the time but blurred and out of focus. He jumped out of bed, no stumbles or weaving thanks to his clean blood stream, and scuttled downstairs.

The concept that your brain can work on solving problems while you sleep was something McQueen had read about in scientific journals for many years. Once your mind is cleared of the many wakeful distractions it can see a way through to solutions. That was the theory, and there had been studies and some evidence of results to back the theory. It was a difficult thing to measure of course, but there was plenty of anecdotal evidence. Edison was said to have harnessed the power of the dream state for some of his best ideas. Whatever it was, McQueen had experienced a revelation, and he was keen to consolidate it as soon as possible.

In a state of some excitement, he opened his laptop where he kept the back-ups of all his recordings. It was one of the early ones he was looking for, and he listened to it twice. He wanted to hear the pitch, tone, and deeper music of the voice, he wanted to get *inside* the voice and listen more closely to the answers it had given. He was more convinced than ever, and he took his notebook back up to bed with him, but didn't sleep. He was waiting for a reasonable hour to make the call he had avoided for years. At six-thirty, he couldn't wait any longer. He was like a kid waiting to wake his parents on Christmas morning. She would be up. She was never a good sleeper, and he knew she went to work quite early, so he wanted to catch her before she left. It had to be today and he hoped she wasn't away.

It wasn't stored on his phone but he could still remember the number. He just hoped it hadn't changed. He typed it in, and after three rings she answered.

'Hi, Julie,' he said trying to sound friendly. 'It's me. How have you been?' There was a longish silence. 'Are you still there?' The conversations you have with people you have shared so much with carry with them so much more than the words alone can convey. For him, at least in this call, there was the embedded innocent happiness and joy of the early years, of the shared struggles and triumphs. But it was all obscured by the brutal hurt and pain of the way it had all ended. *Let's stay friends* had never been an option in their break-up, and he wasn't sure how anyone managed that. He really didn't want to be putting her through this. He didn't want to be forcing himself to do it, but there was no other way. Without knowing it, there was a chance she held a key to the Baxter case, or at least that the house still contained it.

'Yes, I'm here,' answered his ex-wife, and her tone alone was saying, *what the hell do you want*? There were no questions about how he had been or if he was well, but he hadn't expected any. It was completely understandable. How was she supposed to act when her ex-husband came crashing through the phone line into her life after all these years? He thought it best for both of them to get this over with as quickly as possible.

'I'm so sorry to ask this, so I'll get straight to it,' he said. 'You remember I left some boxes in the loft with my old uni notes and papers? You said you were going to bin them all if I didn't collect them. Did you do that?' He closed his eyes and in place of praying hoped really hard.

'No. They're still there,' she said wearily after a few seconds. 'I wasn't deliberately keeping them, by the way. I just never got round to sorting them out. But I will.'

He felt a jolt of relief. If she had disposed of the papers it would have made it all much harder.

'Okay, that's great,' he said, trying to sound casual. 'I really need some of those old notes for something I'm working on, so I can take the boxes off your hands now. Can I come round and pick them all up? There's four, I think?'

She sighed heavily and he could tell she was thinking it through. He wanted to ask how she was and what she'd been up to. He wanted to congratulate her on her new job and tell her how sorry he was it ended the way it did between them,

The Murder Option

but it didn't seem appropriate.

'I'll go up and get them down,' she said.

'Listen, you don't have to do that. I can get them out,' he offered.

'No, I don't want you in my house. I'm working from home this afternoon so I'll put the boxes in the drive, and you can pick them up between four and five. I'll be out then but if they are still there when I get back at six then they are on their way to the tip.' He could sense she was about to hang up.

'Thank you, Julie. I appreciate it. By the way, you'll never believe it but I've given up drinking, for the time being anyway.' He wasn't sure why he'd said that. He wanted to extend the conversation, perhaps, or was it that still, even now, he wanted her approval?

'Good for you,' she answered flatly. 'Ten years too late.' If McQueen had been sticking to the twelve-step addicts' recovery programme, he'd have been apologising to Julie right now for all the past wrongs he'd done. He'd have been admitting and owning all his failings and saying how sorry he was for the way he'd let her down. He would have been listing each particular incident and event where she had suffered because of his drinking. But those words were not going to come from his mouth. He didn't want to say them, and she probably didn't want to hear them. As she had said, it was all a decade too late.

Thirty-three

Sure enough, he found the battered cardboard boxes waiting for him with their layer of loft-dust at the bottom of what was once his drive. He looked up towards the house and its empty windows but saw no signs of movement. It was a relief. If he had seen her, he wasn't sure what he would have done.

He didn't take the boxes to his office because he wanted more floor space than was available there, so he took them home and put them in his living room instead. He made a cup of tea and began sorting through the first box, laying the papers out on the floor in neat rows. The contents were in no particular order, they'd been hurriedly thrown in and weren't even in any chronological sequence. It was a jumble of old lecture notes and copies of marked student papers. It occurred to him that under the latest data protection legislation, what he had there on the floor was probably enough to get him a hefty fine. No one knew he'd kept this stuff, and he'd only done it for personal reference purposes

The Murder Option

that, until now, had never materialised.

As he monotonously flipped his way through the files and documents, scrutinising every one of them for name, date, and title, it flashed through his mind it was the type of repetitive task that would be made less boring by a glass of wine. That's how he'd have done it before. He ignored the idea because he knew from experience alcohol would give him no chance of actually finding what he wanted, and he'd end up having to start all over again the next day.

He was half-way through the third of the four boxes, beginning to lose faith that what he was looking for was really there, when he found it. He pulled out the stapled, dog-eared, photocopied essay by one of his forgotten students and punched the air. A window into the past, a message from a time when such things mattered in a different way to how they mattered now. This theoretical piece had been written to gain marks and approval, and now it was holding the key that would unlock a real murder. He got up from the carpet, where he'd been squatting next to the boxes, and sat on the sofa. He read the essay and read it again, and then he closed his eyes to concentrate on how the pieces fitted together. He'd wanted to see a coherent story develop and now it had.

His phone rang. He was going to ignore it but looked at the display and saw it was a call from Tom. It was just about the only call he would have taken at that moment, but he had made a solemn promise and he had a responsibility.

'Hi. You okay?'

'Not great,' answered the young man in a flat resigned voice, and McQueen's heart sank. Was he calling to say he was lying on a floor somewhere in need of help? It wasn't a good time. McQueen had another mission, but he wasn't about to abandon him.

'What is it, Tom?'

'I wanted you to know my grandmother died yesterday.'

It was not the news he had expected at all and it stunned McQueen a little. It was like the misdirection of a magic trick. While you are watching one hand, the ball is in the other. Even though he could see how old and frail Grace had been, she wasn't the one he'd expected to die first in that family. It must have been what she had in mind when she'd given him that out of character hug when he'd last seen her. She must have been saying goodbye as well as thank you.

'I'm so sorry to hear that, Tom. What happened?'

'Apparently she'd had cancer for some while but she hadn't told anyone. Not me, that's for sure. She'd hidden it from everyone. She was always terrified of hospitals and they told me she had been refusing any medication or chemotherapy. But then she suddenly got very ill. I found her collapsed in her room and I called an ambulance. They took her into hospital, but it was already too late, and she passed away the next day.'

'Sorry,' said McQueen again. 'She was a wonderful woman, full of love for you.'

'At least we had those last weeks together which we wouldn't have had if you'd left me in that flat. I would have found that hard to take. I mean me not being there when she died. So I need to thank you for that.'

McQueen was listening for signs of collapse in Tom himself. He sounded subdued but not overly emotional and encouragingly he sounded sober. As a recovering addict, this was going to be one of those unavoidable life crisis points that would test Tom's resolve and would probably make or break him.

'You don't need to thank me, Tom. It was all down to Grace. I just did what she asked,' said McQueen. 'Are you going to be able to cope now?'

'I think so. I have so far. It's busy. There are things to arrange, family to deal with, and I'm going to do all that for her. I owe her that, but it's going to be hard. It's meant I've had to speak with my parents, and who knows, maybe that's a good thing.'

'I know she really cared about you, Tom, and I think the biggest favour you could do for her memory now is to stay off the drugs and stay alive.' It was a bit of a cheap shot, but McQueen knew the dangers involved in Tom losing his one family supporter. 'I'm going to check in with you every day, Tom, to see how you are doing.'

'You don't need to.'

'Yes, I do. I need to for me. This is as much about me as you. I need your support, and I'm not about to let that go.'

'Okay,' said Tom. 'Well, the other thing I wanted to say is the funeral is next week and I know you're very busy, and I know you weren't related and—'

'I'll be there,' said McQueen.

After he'd finished talking to Tom, he couldn't help his mind flipping to the dirty reality of money and his own financial situation. McQueen hated himself for the thought, but Grace's death was going to have a serious impact on his income. The retainer that paid his rent was gone and Valerie was no longer paying for the Baxter case. Above all, he shouldn't be wasting his time by continuing with a self-funded crusade, but he was too close now to stop.

He took a yellow sticky and made a note which he stuck to the document he'd found in the box, and left them both on the surface in the kitchen. There were some things he needed to know, some history to clear up, and then he was pretty sure he'd be able to talk to Tracey and get her involved. He sent an email to Valerie Baxter.

Hello, Valerie. I'm on my way round to bring the information you wanted. I don't want to post it because there have been some very positive developments and I have a couple of questions only you could answer. You don't need to bother Michael with this at the moment. See you soon.

He considered also sending Tracey an email to tell her he'd be catching up with her later, but decided to make sure he had as much relevant and useful information as possible before he did so. Tracey was the epitome of professionalism and efficiency, and he wanted to give the same impression.

Thirty-four

Driving time had always been good thinking time for McQueen, and on the journey over to see Valerie Baxter his sloppy soup of theories congealed into a mix of solidified concrete. The breakthrough information that had crept into his dreams and then been confirmed by the document he'd found buried amongst his dusty boxes was powerful, but as evidence, it was still circumstantial. Now he needed some hard facts, and they had to start with Valerie. Hers was the name her brother had provided as an alibi, but McQueen had accepted what he'd said without verifying the details. It was like giving someone a job after taking them at their word and without taking up their references. There were other things Valerie could tell him about the day Colin had disappeared, and McQueen wanted to have it all tied up and packaged before he handed it over to Tracey. Knowing his only police contact was battling for credibility with her colleagues, he wanted to give her something tangible and unarguable she could work with. But there was also an element of vanity involved. He wanted to show her he was up to the job, equal to her thorough investigation skills, and a worthy detective partner.

He drove up to the house and parked on the street directly outside the small, metal gate. It squeaked noisily as he pushed it open. He was surprised to find Valerie's front door slightly ajar and stuck to the letter box with Sellotape was a torn piece of lined paper with the words, *come on through to the kitchen*, scrawled across it. He pushed the door a little further open and could see light coming from the kitchen at the end. He called out to warn her it was him and stepped into gloom of the hallway. As he moved forward, he became aware of a presence to his left that had been behind the door, a bulky body. As he started to turn towards it he felt a sharp pain in his leg. He cried out and on instinct struck out at the shadowy person managing to push them away. He stumbled back against the wall. The stinging pain was still in his leg and he could see an empty hypodermic needle jutting out. He grabbed at the plastic tube, pulled it clear, and threw it down.

'Too late,' a male voice said.

Suddenly, his head was swimming and his balance had gone. He tried to focus on whoever had stabbed him with the needle, he knew who it was, but his eyes were blurred, and then he felt himself falling and strong arms eased him to the ground. He was being welcomed back into the smothering blanket of unconsciousness and, as much as he fought it, it was useless. It was closing around him, leaving his world behind, and his last thought was, *is this forever?*

Thirty-five

When McQueen came round, he was sitting up tightly strapped to a chair. He couldn't tell exactly where he was. It had been a dreamless empty passage of time for him, reminiscent of his heart operation when he'd been totally unconscious for hours while fevered activity had gone on all around and inside him. It was the same now. He could remember nothing while his body had been at the mercy of another person.

As his vision cleared, he saw Valerie's brother, Michael Jarvis, sitting in front of him in another straight-backed chair, but he wasn't strapped in, he was leaning forward. He had just administered another injection, presumably to bring McQueen round from the sedation. The back of McQueen's hand stung from the needle.

'It's alright,' he said, smiling. 'You're in safe hands. I trained as a doctor, you know.'

McQueen was trying to get his bearings. It took a few moments for it all to come back to him in terrifying clarity.

There was a flicker of hope, though, he hadn't died, for now at least he was still alive, so Jarvis must have had a reason not to kill him. *Coming here, what a dumb move,* he thought. *I should have gone to Tracey when I found the essay.* Why had he been so adamant he wanted to be sure of his ground before he made any accusations? Vanity. He'd wanted Tracey to see how brilliant he was. He'd needed to speak to Valerie, but it could end up being his fatal mistake.

Feeling slightly sick, he took a deep breath. He was very uncomfortable. His mouth and throat were dry, and his head was pounding. All his joints were screaming out.

There was no point dwelling on what he should have done.

Now all that mattered was staying alive. He ransacked his memory for the hostage strategies he'd studied in the past. Once again, he was about to thrust learned theory through the door into harsh reality to see how it stood up. Scattered phrases came back to him. Try to stay as a human being in your captor's eyes, he remembered. Try to engage them and connect, make it harder for them to think of you as a thing not a person. Try not to show your fear or put yourself in a victim status that some masochists feed off. It was all about buying time now, trying to stay in the game long enough for something to change. For someone to rescue him. 'You're not surprised, are you?' asked Michael. 'That it's me, I mean?'

'No, not really, Michael. But I suppose this finally confirms my conclusions beyond any doubt.'

'You're a clever man, Mr McQueen. Doctor McQueen Ph.D. no less. But you're not even in the same intellectual universe as me. Have you got the slightest understanding of the gravity of the situation you find yourself in?'

'I think so, Michael.'

'But do you realise how lucky you are? I don't think you do, because you are facing the man who will end your life, the person who will extinguish your flame if you want to be poetic about it. Not many people get to know the time and place of their own death like you will. And you will be fulfilling your destiny, the destiny you chose for yourself.'

'Michael, it's not too late. You can be helped.'

'Who's going to help me? *You*? I've been ahead of you, all along. I let you bumble along trying to catch Martin Harper, but I was always watching for signs of danger. Even when you thought you were emailing my sister, you were talking to me. You were giving me warnings without even knowing it. I could tell you were starting to close in on me, that's why I had to act. But I'm very interested to know how you made the vital connection.'

'Yes, you were clever, Michael, and I was lucky. I didn't know for sure, but I had a good idea about what happened. You ran rings round everyone.'

'Don't try to flatter me. It won't work,' snapped Jarvis. 'I don't need your flattery. I know my own potential. Only tell me the facts. I need to know if I left any clues behind.'

'You're right. I wasn't very smart, but last night I suddenly remembered who you were. I had almost recognised you when you first opened the door, but I thought it was because you reminded me of your sister, so I dismissed it. But then I saw your sister's photograph of you in the frame, and that stuck in my head. It came back to me last night. It's the one where you were younger and looked completely different, with your long hair when you were still dying it. And then while I was in a half-dream state, it all came flooding back. You had a different name then, too. You were Mike Mansfield and you sat in my lectures for a few months, didn't you? Until you dropped out.'

Jarvis laughed.

'I didn't drop out. I made a deliberate career decision and moved to medicine, but well done, Mr McQueen. And yes, you're right, I went by my dead father's name back then, the name my sister and I had both grown up with. A terrible name really, a daily reminder but now I use my mother's family name.' He sat contemplating McQueen for a few moments.

'Unlike you, I have a perfect memory. I forget nothing and no one,' he said.

Narcissism, thought McQueen. *He's showing off even though his audience is one captured man. He needs me to know how brilliant he's been.*

'When you came to see me that first time, I recognised you straight away,' continued Jarvis. 'Of course I had the advantage that I knew you from the days when I had seen you standing alone, strutting and showing off for cheap laughs at the lectern. I had listened to your droning lectures and tried to keep my eyes open, so it was easier for me to have that memory.'

Even then he was jealous that what he saw as an inferior intellect was the centre of attention.

'I wanted my sister to make the police catch David Harper. But I didn't know it was you she'd hire. I have to

The Murder Option

admit I was a tiny bit worried you'd spot me, but I could see when you looked at me, you had no idea who I was.'

He was offended he hadn't been recognised, even though he didn't want to be found out.

'You were always too sozzled to take in who your students were back then, anyway. Old, muddled McQueen we used to call you. The rumour was that you'd died of a heart attack, by the way.'

He was trying to attack and belittle McQueen, to make him a lesser being, to justify his actions of removing an insignificant roadblock.

'Sorry to disappoint you, Michael, but I survived that one.'

'So it appears. Anyway, let's get back to the facts. You suddenly remembered me, but then what?'

'It woke me up in more ways than one, Michael, and I went back into my files. I always kept the papers that showed outstanding talent. Yours was exceptional. It took me a while, but I found your essay about your perfect murder. I still have it. I gave you ninety-three percent at the time. In the essay you say that, in your view, the perfect murder isn't just one where the murderer gets away with it, the murderer also has to make sure an enemy takes all the blame. That way it's two birds with one stone, as you put it. And then you detailed an example. That example as we both know has now become reality, it was like reading the case notes to your brother-in-law's death. The enemy you had was Martin Harper, and he was the one you planned to take the blame. He should have taken the rap, as they say.'

'He would have done, too. I left plenty of subtle clues at

the scene. I was relying on the forensic teams and the labs to pick up the DNA. You might be interested to know I got Harper's DNA from his bins. I ferreted like a tabloid journalist and got enough of him, hairs and yukky things to easily convict him, but then that utter moron farmer destroyed everything.'

Jarvis was getting a little agitated now, but was still talking. 'Anyway,' he said, 'I don't want anyone to spot your car outside, so I'm going to hide it. We'll chat later. I'm very keen to hear what you knew and how clever you really were. I need to know any mistakes I might have made. Don't go away. Oh, and the essay. Did you bring it? And all the evidence I asked for? Is it in the car?'

'No, it's all at my office,' lied McQueen. He was thinking that if Jarvis killed him, but didn't find the essay because it was still at his flat, the police might find it and follow the trail and be able to work out what had happened. He had confidence Tracey Bingham would be able to put two and two together, if they let her near it. It was a desperate avenue of how to leave a damning signal from his grave, like a message written in blood on a wall by a victim.

'Well, we're going to have to get those back at some point,' said Jarvis. 'But we'll get to that. For now, let's deal with the car.'

As Jarvis went out, McQueen glimpsed a corridor beyond him and then heard him go down some stairs. So McQueen was in an upstairs room, very possibly in Valerie Baxter's house. His prison was probably an unused bedroom, but there was no furniture anywhere other than the two chairs and a small table by the door. Considering the clutter

The Murder Option

of the rest of the house, the emptiness of this room was stark. It must have meant that even if it was in her house, she was never allowed in the room. On the table were some small items, and McQueen guessed they were from his own pockets because that's where Jarvis had picked up his car keys. Was his phone there? He couldn't see it. He could just about make out the tiny dot of white that was the snowy peak on the lid of his expensive pen. His present from Julie. Bizarrely, he wondered what would happen to it once he was gone. Would Jarvis use it, sell it, or throw it away? He recognised his mind was straying and pulled himself back to the here and now.

The window was blacked out with a blind, but if he could shuffle over to it maybe he could break it and shout for help. He tried to rock his seat but could not move even a fraction. The chair was heavy and solid, and every part of him was tightly taped to it. Even his head was held in place somehow. He'd have to get Jarvis to loosen the tape if he was going to attempt anything. And where *was* Valerie Baxter? He thought she'd been downstairs in the kitchen, but he hadn't actually seen her when he'd looked down the corridor before being jumped by Michael in the hallway. Was she in on this? He found it hard to believe she was party to this madness but anything was possible.

McQueen's eyes darted around the room looking for any tiny hint of an escape. He saw none. He needed to keep his mind working, to stave off the fear and panic that was threatening to engulf him, and turn his thought processes into mush.

He wasn't dead yet and as far as he could see that was

because Michael Jarvis wanted to be sure there was no one else following behind him in his footsteps. Should he pretend there was? Would it help to keep him alive, or would it force his captor's hand to get rid of him?

And there was another element to this. Sure, Jarvis wanted to know if there were any glaring signposts he'd left, but he also wanted to parade his achievements in front of a man who'd been his lecturer. He wanted approval from the man he planned to kill. He wanted to be patted on the back and told how clever he'd been by a person with qualifications he himself had never achieved, but at the same time he wanted to show McQueen how stupid he was and diminish him to the level of a valueless mosquito to be squashed.

Cognitive dissonance, thought McQueen. *When the brain tries to hold two contradictory ideas at the same time it causes psychological stress and causes the person to do all they can to resolve the conflict.* It was a huge area of psychological study. McQueen tried to focus on that to bring his mind back under control. Either Jarvis was going to decide McQueen was an idiot not worthy of respect and kill him, or he was going to decide he shouldn't harm such a learned man.

His mind wandering again. McQueen remembered famously, Benjamin Franklin had used the theory without knowing it in a phenomenon that became known as the Ben Franklin Effect. Franklin had used it to make an enemy into a friend, but McQueen couldn't remember the details. Basically, it meant if you could get a person who didn't like you to do you a favour, then praised them, it caused such psychological conflict within them that they would decide they did like you rather than living with the idea that they had helped someone they hated. It was a long shot, ask Jarvis for a favour and then hope his already ruptured mind flip-flopped into liking McQueen enough to spare him. It was ridiculous, and McQueen could feel his hope draining away.

He tried again to rock the chair and tears of frustration and fear started to bubble in his eyes. He wasn't sure he'd ever thought about how his end would come, but it wasn't like this. It was no use, his thoughts zig-zagged like frightened birds from a tree and he was left with only an anxious swirl of emotion.

Thirty-six

When Jarvis returned, he dropped McQueen's car keys onto the table, obviously satisfied with himself.

'No one will find it there,' he said, without explaining. 'Did you try to move?' he asked with a grin. 'Did you think you could escape? I bet you did. Did you work out the chair is screwed to the floor so you can't tip it?'

'Michael, I really need to use the toilet,' said McQueen, hoping that if nothing else once the tape had been removed it would give him an opportunity to escape.

Jarvis nodded. 'Be my guest,' he said. 'Do what you must right there. You are positioned above a plastic sheet precisely for that purpose. You aren't going to be alive long enough for it to make any difference. I mean, you don't have to worry about chaffing or soreness or anything like that. And I have anosmia. Do you know what that means? It means I have no sense of smell, never have, which can be a big bonus sometimes. Times such as this,' he said with the sweetest smile.

The Murder Option

'Now, you've told me about my essay, but do you remember what your example of a perfect murder was? Because I do,' asked Jarvis. He didn't wait for the answer. 'I'll tell you. You said taking the victim out to sea on a boat was the perfect place to kill and dispose of a body. Do you remember that?'

'I do.'

'You said it must happen all the time, well, as you might have gathered I'm very keen on symbolism, I like things to have meaning. When something has a symmetry and a deep meaning it resonates with the cosmos. The meaning itself adds power to the action. Stabbed in the back, for instance? That was very meaningful to me. And now there's you, and to make your life come round neatly in a meaningful circle, I've arranged something for you. It's your own choice of murder. I'm going to sedate you again. It's safe. I know what I'm doing, and then I will put you in a large holdall and put you in my van. You'll be interested to know that it's the same vehicle Colin took his last ride in. You see, meaningful, it all adds power to the cause. Now, you are heavy, but I carried you up the stairs so I know I can do it. We're going to drive to the east coast, it takes about two hours from here, and I have use of a boat. Yes, I actually hired a boat in your honour, and we are going to go for a little sea trip, but you are not going to come back. I want you to experience the end. I will revive you, and still alive but helpless, I will let you tragically slip overboard. On a physical and spiritual level you will feel the swell of the waves as you slip beneath them. Your soul will know, McQueen. Your soul will know you have returned to the thing you dreamed. The same as Colin's soul knew his death was fitting and meaningful.

'You may be wondering why I would go to all that trouble. I think it's because, at heart, I'm a romantic. I love the idea you will die in that manner. After boring us all with your vision of a perfect murder in the lecture, it will be granted by me. It's perfect.'

McQueen tried hard to swallow but his mouth was too dry. Jarvis couldn't have known, but ever since he was a child he'd had a morbid fear of drowning. It was not only his so-called perfect murder, it was also his terrifying nightmare. It had been forged as a powerful fear as a young teenager in the town's swimming baths when two older boys had held him under at the deep end. They had pushed him down playfully as if it were all an innocuous game they called 'submarines', but then when he started to try to surface strong hands had gripped his head and pushed harder. It was certainly bullying, but he'd never known if they'd really meant to drown him. The panic he'd felt as his lungs began to strain and hurt had taken full control of him. The need for oxygen was so elemental that it overrode everything. A deep lying animal survival instinct had given him a burst of desperate strength and he'd managed to flail and kick his way clear. He'd grabbed the side of the pool, hauled himself up, and lay gasping while the boys had swum off, laughing. The lifeguard carried on reading his magazine in his chair, believing they were just playing. The drowning sensation had never left him. It had visited him in dreams and kept him out of the deep waves on holiday. And now, in full waking consciousness, it swept over him again. He needed to push the terror away. He tried to concentrate on Jarvis.

Grandiose, he thought, another one of the psychopath's tickboxes.

'I did think it at the time you gave that lecture, how fitting it would be for you to die like that, but I never really believed my dream would come true. And yet, here we are. It's fate.'

McQueen felt the tightness of the tape across his chest and the inevitability of his death, and he was suddenly seized with the same uncontrollable panic he'd felt under the water. He had a desperate urge to appeal for mercy and plead for his life, but he knew it was what Jarvis wanted to hear and it would go no way towards saving him. Shamefully he felt the hot spread of urine seeping through his trousers and he could hear it drip onto the plastic beneath him. It was the physical manifestation of his helplessness, and a sign of how desperate his situation was.

'Oh dear,' said Jarvis wrinkling his nose with a look of distain. 'The great, great, great, mighty, mighty Doctor McQueen has pissed himself like a child,' and then he laughed.

Without wanting to, McQueen was fulfilling his victim role for Jarvis who was gaining his perverse power from that control. McQueen was close to completely losing it, so he closed his eyes and thought of something a friend had once told him. The guy was a serious rock climber and he'd said one of the skills of dangerous climbing was managing to banish all panic. If you panic on a rock face you can make stupid decisions and you can die. You have to learn to put all thoughts of the plunge below you to the back of your mind and concentrate on one thing, the next handhold. Keep him talking was McQueen's next handhold, his only option.

'Does Valerie know about all this?' he asked. There was a flash of anger on Michael's face at the mention of his sister.

'Leave her out of this,' he said irritably. He went back over to the table, opened a small bag, and took out a hypodermic. 'Impress me,' he said. 'Tell me what you think you know and I'll help you fill in the blanks. You can think of it as me marking your work. Let's see if you pass.'

McQueen had nothing to lose. He didn't have much, only a lot of assumptions and guesswork but he had to go with it, he was already losing this battle to stay alive.

'Okay. From the beginning?'

'Please.'

'Well, okay. Let's go right back. Both you and your sister have mentioned your tough upbringing. I'm going to say you had an abusive father.' McQueen could tell by the flinch Michael gave that he'd been correct. 'He abused Valerie, and you were too young to do anything protect her.'

'Or myself,' interjected Michael quietly.

'You were young and powerless, and that powerlessness in the face of his behaviour deeply affected you. He probably abused your mother as well, so she couldn't help.'

'As good as killed her. She was timid and easily bullied, a lot like my sister, and she couldn't take it in the end. She killed herself, she drank a concoction of kitchen products from under the sink one day, and died a horrible painful death being burnt out from the inside. I came home from school and there she was on the kitchen floor. The doctor wrote that the contorted look on her face was quite horrific, but I didn't feel horrified. Do you know what I felt,

McQueen?'

The first answers that came to his mind were anger or guilt, but then he put it in the context of who Michael Jarvis was. He dredged up memories of the studies he'd read about the formative years of psychopaths.

'Curiosity?'

Michael beamed with joy. 'Exactly! Well done. Yes, I stood looking at my mother lying there for a long time, trying to work out what the real difference was between how she was and how she'd been that morning. It was fascinating.'

'I'm sorry for you, Michael. That's an awful thing to happen to a child. It must have affected you deeply.'

Jarvis had cocked his head to one side, his eyes as black and unfathomable as a bird's as he studied McQueen.

'Are you trying to be sympathetic to make me like you?' he asked, not waiting for an answer. 'You're pathetic. In her death, my mother gave me something. She gave me the gift of an option. She gave me the option of suicide as a viable alternative to a bad life. It was something I thought about from time to time but, as you know, it was an option I rejected in favour of a better one. So keep going, McQueen. You aren't doing very well at the moment.'

'You said your father was dead, and you said you changed your name from his, so based on what I already know you're capable of, I'm going to assume that to protect you and your sister you killed him.'

Jarvis clapped his hands gleefully. 'Excellent,' he said. 'But officially it was a terrible accident with an electric lawnmower,' he added with a sick little smile. 'Or at least it looked like an accident to the police, and no one suspected a thing. In fact, we got a lot of sympathy for that. Everyone was so kind to us both which made it even more delicious.'

Jarvis was sitting back down in front of him, syringe in hand.

'Right,' said McQueen. 'So from that successful action you learned a valuable lesson. The best way to protect your sister was through murder. Your impressionable mind was moulded forever. It became the option of choice for you.'

'Yes, the murder option,' grinned Jarvis. 'Can you imagine how thrilled I was when I saw that come up as one of the topics on your lecture list? It was another one of your interminable lectures I sat through knowing all the time you were speaking that I knew more about the subject than you. I liked the title, though. What can I say? It resonated with me. Now, carry on with your insights.'

'The years go by but, regrettably, you don't become a doctor. You said it was the exams that caught you out, but I think maybe there was some sort of disciplinary incident.'

'A minor incident completely blown out of all proportion by the university. They over reacted and to be honest, at that point, I'd lost all respect for them anyway.'

McQueen saw a terrible prospect opening up before him and he couldn't stop himself from exploring it like the tongue that won't leave the broken tooth alone.

'While we're filling in the blanks, Michael, can I ask, did someone die in this incident by any chance?'

He laughed. 'Yes, I'm afraid so. It's a long story, but we shared a flat, and he was a type one diabetic, and it's so easy for insulin dosing to go fatally wrong. Anyway, to be honest, he was a complete dullard. He would never have been a good doctor. I did watch him die, and I didn't try to save him, but I saved many future patients from his incompetence. They preach standards a lot when you are learning to be a doctor, but they have no understanding of real standards. But no matter, please keep going, *Doctor* McQueen, though I hope I don't hurt your feelings when I say that you, too, just like me, are not a real doctor.' He said the word doctor with a deep-seated resentful venom.

McQueen breathed deeply and continued. He was struggling to keep his mind on track.

'Er, so, let's see, frustrated and feeling that you haven't been respected or rewarded for your superior intellect, you struggle to find your niche in life. I don't know if you kill anyone else over the years?' He looked at Jarvis for confirmation who stared back non-committedly. McQueen ploughed on. 'You have various jobs, but none of them quite work out. You're not good with authority, you make rash decisions, you think everyone else is a fool so you find it hard to get on with bosses and you find it hard to stick to mundane tasks you see no value in. Unfortunately, that's what most jobs are made up of, so employment is tricky for you. And then fast forward to you becoming a consultant. Finally, you've found something you are pretty good at, something that gives you the opportunity to show how clever you are, but then Colin puts you in touch with Martin Harper.'

'Ah, yes, we get to the legendary Martin Harper, all around Superman.'

'Unfortunately, Harper is his own man, and he doesn't

agree with your advice. He doesn't give you a job, maybe even ridicules you which reawakens your feelings of inadequacy and failure.' Jarvis raised an eyebrow at the word inadequacy but didn't interrupt.

'So Harper becomes your new enemy. You are incensed he hasn't recognised your genius, and you plot revenge. At first you try to discredit and ruin his company with the fly-tipping story, but it's clumsy. Shane Daley is too stupid and too easily found out, and Harper and his company get away unscathed. But there I have a question. Can you fill in another blank for me, Michael?' asked McQueen. 'How did you actually do that? How did you get the truck and how did you find Shane? You've beaten me on that one.' *Let him parade his cleverness*, thought McQueen. *Keep it going as long as possible, while he's talking he's not killing.*

Jarvis didn't hesitate. 'Colin used to work from home every Friday and this room that you are so comfortably sitting in used to be his office, before I cleared it out and sanitised it, that is. His desk, which stood there,' he gestured, 'was full of useful information about Harper Engineering and especially their transport operations. Colin brought things home he probably never should have, I even found a selection of spare keys here. It was easy.'

'And Shane?'

'Ah, Shane. Have you heard of the dark web, Doctor McQueen?'

'Of course.' Some of McQueen's work called for him to trawl through the sewer of the dark web. Jarvis was referring to the nefarious hidden parts of the internet sitting on private servers and not accessible to normal search engines.

The Murder Option

'You can get anything and everything if you know where to look,' he said proudly. 'It's where I get my medical supplies from, by the way.'

He showed McQueen the syringe and then waved his hands impatiently for his captive to continue.

'Well, when that didn't work you probably had other plans for Harper, maybe even murder, but then one day Valerie comes to you crying. Colin has found out about her affair with Martin Harper. It was a mistake, but far from forgiving her as she maintained to me, Colin has started to, what, mentally abuse her? Hit her? She turns to the person she always turns to at times like this, her brother protector. You decide it's high time this backstabber is taught a lesson and, at the same time, you can make Harper suffer by framing him for the murder.

'One morning you pick up Colin as he walks to the station and you take him somewhere and kill him. Your medical training allowed you to make a perfect single stab through his back and heart. I would think it was as he was walking ahead of you.'

'Not quite,' interjected Jarvis. 'I asked him to help me pick up a heavy sack in the back of my van, and then when he was leaning forward, I struck.'

'Right, I see. So then he's in the van, and then you dump him in that field as yet another connection to Harper, hoping the police will put it together with the DNA and arrest him. But they don't. They don't even officially question him and it turns out it's because he has an alibi. Tell me, why a clever man like you didn't you think of that, Michael? It seems like a stupid error on your part.'

Jarvis bristled with anger. It was risky to annoy him, but McQueen had to try to break the helpless victim role he had assumed. He had to try to disturb the control that Jarvis had and take some control back himself.

'It wasn't an error. I had thought of it. He wasn't supposed to have an alibi that morning because I'd arranged for him to meet a mystery client. There was no client, of course, and he wouldn't have been able to prove where he was, but he didn't show up.'

'Yes, turns out he ditched your fake client for a real-life woman. A well-connected woman, as it happened. Meanwhile, the police had missed all your clever clues, and they went chasing the wrong man. Bainbridge.'

He looked at Jarvis who had been nodding rhythmically along.

'You're not as clever as you think you are, McQueen. You got one thing wrong so far,' said Jarvis. 'I'm disappointed in you. I think you're looking at a fail on this paper.'

'Really?' said McQueen. 'Show me where I made a mistake.' As most of what he'd said was based on educated guesses, he wasn't surprised that not all of it was accurate, but he wanted to keep Jarvis talking.

'Do you really think Valerie is the type of woman to have an affair with a snake like Harper? She is a loyal and loving person. She was a devoted wife, but Colin offered her to Harper like a bag of sweets. Her husband actually took her devotion and stabbed her in the back. He offered his wife, my sister, as a sexual gift, in order to keep his job. They are both pigs, those men. I'd always thought Colin was alright in

The Murder Option

a dull sort of way, but when Harper was thinking of getting rid of him, Colin knew he'd always had a thing for Val, and he did that vile thing. He wasn't leaving to join any competitor, he was being sacked. She was too innocent. She had too much loyalty. She was too damaged to refuse.'

Jarvis was right. McQueen hadn't seen that coming and he had to admit an affair had seemed out of character for Valerie Baxter even though she had admitted it. McQueen saw a chance to offer Jarvis a lifeline, and perhaps make one of his own.

'These are mitigating circumstances,' he said, sympathetically. 'The pain you've both endured would play very well with a jury, it might...'

But Jarvis wasn't listening.

'Forget it. There's never going to be a jury,' he said. 'Keep going, unless you're finished in which case we have somewhere to be.' McQueen tried to shake his head to clear it but couldn't. *Where to next?* he wondered.

'Bainbridge,' continued McQueen, suddenly. 'You already had a grudge against him for destroying the DNA evidence and with it your plans. When I told Valerie the farmer had something to tell me, she was the only one I told, and she must have told you. You went over there before me and with his own shotgun made Bainbridge tell you what he'd seen.'

'Yes, that's right. And do you know what it was? All it was, was a tissue caught in the fence. It might have been one of mine that had blown out of my pocket when I was dumping colin. If it was mine, it might still have my DNA on it, so it was a risk factor and just as well I didn't let you find it.'

'Bainbridge told you what to look for?'

'Yes, he was a very stubborn man. He resisted my questions. To begin with, I told him you weren't coming and that you had sent me instead, but he didn't believe me. The gun was right there, propped up in the corner of the kitchen, almost waiting for me, and I find most people lose their stubbornness when they are faced with their own death.'

'And then you shot him in the mouth and tried to make it look like a suicide.'

'Tried? The police believed it.'

'Not all of them, but anyway, after murdering him you went up to the field. You were wearing your Cragtops walking boots, by the way. You found the tissue, saw that it could be a risk, and took it.'

'My Cragtops? That is impressive, McQueen. Well done. Was it the footprints?' Jarvis said it patronisingly, thinking it had no bearing on anything now. 'Perhaps I should get rid of those. Thank you for the tip-off.'

'I can't take credit for that detection work, I'm afraid. It wasn't me who worked out what boots they were. It was a police detective called Tracey Bingham who I've been collaborating with all along.'

'Fortunately, I know you're lying. You don't have a very good relationship with the police, you told me that yourself.'

'Tracey is different. She came to me off the record because she doesn't want to let this case drop. She knows everything. I've shared it all. If you kill me, it only adds to the charges. That's why I think you should turn yourself in and make it easier.' McQueen was studying Michael to see if the threat of Tracey was having any impact, but he seemed to be ignoring it.

'I seriously doubt that, McQueen,' he said casually. 'And if you don't mind me saying, it's a bit of a pathetic attempt at saving yourself from a man as supposedly intelligent as you. You're trying to make me think the police wolves are at my door and it would be better for me if I let you live. It won't work.' He started to fill the needle.

'So tell me,' said McQueen, trying another tack. 'You can help me out here as well. Was it you who sent down the hay bales in Bainbridge's barn?'

Jarvis laughed at the memory.

'Yes, it was, but that one was a complete accident, and I must apologise for that.'

'Did you follow me there?'

'No, don't be an idiot. I was already there. Just like you, it had occurred to me that the gormless farmer might have something more to say now the police weren't hounding him. He was a loose cannon. There was no telling what he might come up with, and I didn't really want you talking to him and finding anything new out. I went over there to poke around and maybe to speak to him. I parked a mile away and walked there, and I'd just got to his yard, and that's when I saw you show up. I ducked in the barn because i didn't want you to see me there. It would have looked very suspicious, so I went inside, and was watching through a crack in the door. I saw you didn't go in the house and I heard you shouting and obviously you never got to talk to him. You were about to go and then stupidly you started to come over to the barn. I knew you were going to come in and, as I say, I didn't want you to see me so I climbed up the bales. I really didn't intend to push them down on you. I didn't think you were much of a threat at that stage, but when you came in one started to tip over under my feet, so I thought what the hell and pushed the rest. You were buried under them and it gave me the perfect chance to get away. I didn't think it would kill you, but if it had, so what?'

McQueen was desperately trying to think of something else to say, but his mind had gone blank in the face of his impending death.

'And so you see, I've always been ahead of you, even way back before you even realise.'

What did he mean? McQueen's brain flashed to a psychological profile, written long ago, he had come across as he had worked his way through the boxes in his house.

'Connolly,' he said. 'Marion Connolly.' Jarvis looked at him open-mouthed.

'You killed Marion Connolly. She was your tutor for one of your modules. She was a harsh critic. She didn't suffer fools, and she believed in tough love. She absolutely humiliated you in one of her lectures. You couldn't stand that, so you killed her in the car park.' McQueen had stitched together some wild guesses. He didn't even know for sure that Jarvis had even been in Marion's lectures, but it was all he had.

The two men stared at each other, both knowing in that instant of eye contact it was true. McQueen had remembered his profile, the one the police had dismissed at the time and he could see now how it fitted Jarvis. He'd taken a desperate shot in the dark, but it seemed to have hit home.

'How?' asked Jarvis, visibly stunned for the first time.

'Detective Tracey Bingham,' lied McQueen. 'She's on that cold case and she read my psychological profile. She's going through old DNA evidence right now. It's only a matter of time.' Jarvis paused. Finally McQueen had broken through his air of superiority.

'And how was that meaningful?' asked McQueen. 'Murdering a person who was much, much more intelligent than you.'

'I bludgeoned her,' answered Jarvis simply and recomposed he began smiling again. 'She had verbally bludgeoned me in the lecture for daring to disagree with her. She beat me with words in front of everyone, so I paid her back. Her soul understood that. And by the way, there was no DNA evidence, I made sure of that. If the policewoman had really been looking at it as a cold case, she would have known that. So, you see, you're caught in a lie, Mr McQueen.'

There was a noise from downstairs, a door opening, and McQueen heard Valerie Baxter's voice calling for Michael. Before Jarvis could stop him, McQueen shouted out.

'Up here, Valerie! Help me! We're up here.'

McQueen was sure Jarvis would clamp his hand over his mouth to stop him yelling, but he didn't do anything except lean back in his chair. After hearing the feet on the stairs, there was a terrible few seconds where nothing happened, and Michael Jarvis looked into his face. Eventually the door opened and Valerie came in. McQueen felt a flood of relief when he saw her and the look of horror on her face.

'What's going on?' she asked her brother.

'I'm taking care of things, Val,' said Michael. 'I always do.' Jarvis still wasn't trying to stop McQueen from speaking, so he decided to go for broke with some brutal truths for Valerie, his saviour.

'Valerie, it was your brother who killed your husband. It wasn't Martin Harper at all. It was Michael. He wanted to protect you and he wanted you to frame Harper. And since then, another innocent man has died, the farmer, Peter Bainbridge.' Surprisingly Jarvis didn't seem at all bothered by McQueen's accusations. He had an air of supreme confidence, and Valerie was just standing staring at McQueen.

'Do you hear what I'm saying? It was Michael. He is ill and he needs help, Valerie. Now he wants to kill me. Do you want my death on your hands?'

She was taking it all in, the man taped to the chair in front of her and the pool of urine that was spread and stinking beneath him. She blinked a few times before speaking.

'I know Michael killed Colin. I didn't ask him to do it, but I understood why it had to happen. Michael has always done the right thing for us and he is much cleverer than me. The police should have arrested Martin Harper, but they never did. That's why I hired you. I thought it would be good you were never a policeman, but you wouldn't do it, would you?'

McQueen felt like not just the rug but the whole carpet had been yanked from beneath him. He could see she was profoundly broken and wasn't going to be any help to him. The purposeful glow he had first recognised in her was gone.

The Murder Option

She was transformed in the presence of her brother into a shell of the person he thought he knew.

'If Michael thinks it's the right thing to do, then it must be,' she said.

'But I've never done anything to you, Valerie.'

'He wants to put me in prison, Val,' said Jarvis. 'And if I go to prison or one of his hospitals, which are just the same as a prison, then you will be on your own, Val. And I can't let that happen. I need to be here to protect you, you know that.'

'Think about it,' said McQueen to the lost and overwhelmed woman. 'You've never hurt anyone and now this will be on you. My murder will be down to you.'

'You should have made them arrest Martin Harper and then all of this would have been alright,' she said as she crossed the room. 'It's your own fault.'

'Okay, what if I tell you I will help you convict Martin Harper now?' said McQueen desperately. 'I have evidence, and I can make that happen.'

'Pathetic,' said Michael, and he was right.

As Valerie started to open the door to the corridor, they all heard the loud jangle of the front door bell. Valerie stood frozen and Michael went to the blind and pulled it aside enough to see out.

'It's alright, it's a woman. Looks a like market researcher or something,' he said. 'Let's leave her outside and she'll go away.'

McQueen's heart was racing. Should he shout? Would they hear from outside with him up here? It was his only chance, but as he started to yell, Jarvis grabbed his mouth choking off the sound.

'Get the tape from the table,' he snapped at Valerie, and she hurried to get the roll he had used to bind McQueen to the chair. 'Tear off a strip,' he ordered and she dutifully obeyed. McQueen could see the little girl she had become right before his eyes, doing everything her big brother told her to. Jarvis roughly slapped the tape over McQueen's mouth to muffle his cries for help.

The ringing continued, and then there were loud, increasingly violent bangs on the door. Whoever it was wasn't going away and it was starting to become an attention attracting annoyance to Michael. Presumably, he was thinking of Valerie's neighbours. McQueen reasoned they would have to answer the door, and he was waiting to see if he would jam that needle into his arm first because if he did, it was game over. McQueen could imagine the person outside listening to hear if anyone was responding to their knocking. Could it be Tracey? It had to be, didn't it? In desperation, so close to an escape, he tried to shout, but he had been effectively silenced by the sticky gag. Valerie was standing to one side watching with wide frightened eyes. Then Michael spoke with a father's commanding voice to Valerie.

'You go down and tell her to go away. I'll sort this out.' Obediently she went out. McQueen knew he was now merely a logistical problem for Jarvis. He could see he had lost his human status in Jarvis' eyes and there was little chance of regaining it. Valerie hadn't returned, and McQueen knew his last hope was probably gone.

'You've said all you need to say. I know everything I need to know.'

The Murder Option

He sat back in his chair and held up the hypodermic. He tapped it expertly to remove any dangerous air bubbles. *Force of habit* guessed McQueen, bitterly he wondered if he would he swab his arm with disinfectant too.

'I'm going to keep you under while we get out to sea so you can't cause any fuss, and then, as I said, you will awaken and your soul will experience the full glory of being in your own personal murder. It's an exciting day for you.'

Downstairs there were still voices and then the sounds of a hurried climbing of the stairs. Valerie came back in. She looked alarmed and terrified.

'She says she is a police detective,' she gushed. 'She knows who I am, and she asked about you. She's looking for him.' With wild eyes she pointed at McQueen who was still trying to shout through the tape. 'She wants to come in and look around.'

'Is she alone?' asked Michael with disturbing calmness.

'Yes.'

'In that case, I think she must be off duty and being nosey. The police never travel alone when they are working. Take her into the kitchen.' Valerie went out and Jarvis showed McQueen the syringe again.

'I've got more, don't worry, but I think perhaps you might have a friend along for your final sea trip,' he said, and then taking the full hypodermic went out of the door leaving it slightly open.

McQueen was frantic. He struggled with all his strength against the bindings which were cutting in to his arms but weren't shifting. He spat and tried to bite the tape on his face and pushed his tongue against it as hard as he could. His jerking had freed up his head just a little and he was able to shake it like a dog with a toy in its jaws. He felt something give as the combination of the wet of his mouth and the movement dislodged the side of the tape across his mouth.

'Tracey!' he screamed. 'He's going to stab you. Watch out, watch out, he has a needle!' he yelled over and over again through the sand-paper dryness of his throat. Downstairs he could hear noises, the sounds of a scuffle. Out of breath, tears streaming down his face, he continued to writhe and yell. Eventually, exhausted, he stopped for a second and listened. He heard the sound of footsteps on the stairs again. *Please let it be Tracey*, he prayed, but it wasn't. Valerie came into the room. She stood in front of him glassy-eyed, rims red with tears.

'The policewoman tried to hurt Michael,' she said pathetically. 'She bent his arm and tried to make him cry. He needed my help.'

'What did you do, Valerie?" asked McQueen gently. 'What happened?'

'I couldn't let her hurt Michael, could I? It was like Daddy. I tried to push her off and I told her to stop but she was too strong, so I got the chopping board, the big heavy one that Colin bought, and I lifted it up and dropped it on her head. Then she fell off Michael. But it's okay, Michael's taking care of her now. It's alright, he's a doctor. He's given her something to help her sleep.'

McQueen knew he only had a few moments now before Jarvis would be back and he felt his only chance was Valerie. She was the weak spot in Michael's plans.

'Come on, Valerie,' he said softly. 'It's going to be okay.

The Murder Option

Come and take some of this tape off so I can help Michael. He needs my help now.'

Valerie was standing in a zombie-like state, her eyes unblinking as her shattered mind tried to cope with the events that had unfolded around her.

'I couldn't do that,' she said in a shaky voice. 'Michael wouldn't like it.'

'Come on, Valerie,' he coaxed. 'It's going to be okay. Really, it's all going to be fine. Just get the tape off my wrists. Once I'm free I can make sure Michael is alright. I won't let anyone harm him.'

'That's very nice of you,' said Michael from the doorway and McQueen's hopes faded into the distance like a half-remembered dream you chase and chase but never catch. 'Nice that you'd be thinking of me and my welfare.' He came into the room and McQueen could see the syringe in his hand was empty.

'She's a policewoman,' spluttered McQueen. 'She will have called for back-up before she came in. Your only chance now is to give up, Michael. Don't make it worse than it already is.'

'I don't think so,' said Jarvis, taking a new ampule from his little bag. He was brusque and business-like now. His encounter with Tracey had clearly made him decide not to waste any more time. Valerie was standing to one side, motionless. 'She was off duty; I doubt if she was even supposed to be here. By the time anyone comes to ask about her, both of you will be long gone. I've already moved her car.' He punctured the top of the small bottle and refilled his syringe, then came back over to his chair and sat in front of

McQueen. His eyes seemed to have deepened in colour, they were almost black and devoid of humanity. 'By rights, you shouldn't be sharing needles,' he said. 'Quite a dangerous thing to do. But given the circumstances, I don't think you need to worry about it.'

McQueen's arms were taped to the side of the chair and Jarvis pushed up his sleeve. McQueen tried to wriggle, anything to make it harder for him but it was useless.

'Stop, Michael. Please, don't do it,' said McQueen, but the efficient taker of lives wasn't listening. The needle stung his forearm, and within seconds he could feel his mental grip on everything loosening. The panic-induced adrenaline was trying to combat the powerful drug in his veins, but it was an unfair fight. In hospital they ask you to count down from ten, and McQueen would have probably reached six before the black, bottomless pit of unconsciousness swallowed him up.

Thirty-seven

It took at least two minutes before McQueen could work out where he was. His memory had fragmented and the discomfort in his body further added to his confusion. He was lying on his back. It was dark. Something was close to his face, and his body was swaying, being pushed and pulled back and forth by gravity. He could feel the sound of the steady rhythmic throbbing of an engine reverberating through his bones. He was travelling. He tried to move, but his hands were fastened behind his back, and the pain in his shoulders and bent knees was excruciating. As his mind slowly returned to a version of its functioning capacity with a growing dread, he could start to work it out. The rocking movements that kept leaving his stomach behind were unmistakable. He was on a boat and he was inside something, a bag or sack. A combination of the lurching motion and the after-effects of the drug were making him feel extremely sick. He had nothing to lose so started to shout for help. A few seconds later there was the rasping sound of a zip followed by a shaft of blinding light. When he could finally focus, he saw the smiling face of Michael Jarvis looking down at him.

'You can shout as much as you like,' said Jarvis. 'You don't need a gag anymore because there is no one around to hear you. You have woken in time to enjoy your perfect murder,' he continued. 'I hope you're impressed with my medical skills. I estimated the anaesthetic dose perfectly.' He continued to unzip what must have been a large holdall type bag and then roughly rolled McQueen out of it onto the deck. A salty spray reached McQueen's face helping to revive him slightly as the boat dipped and splashed forward.

'She,' said Jarvis pointing at another large black holdall, possibly a tent bag, 'Mrs Meddler, doesn't need to wake up. She's smaller than you, less bodyweight, and I gave her a bigger dose, so she will go to her watery end sleeping peacefully. But then this isn't her idea, you see. It isn't her perfection. You brought her into yours.' He leaned over the other bag, unzipped it, and rolled an unconscious Tracey Bingham out next to McQueen. He looked at her face for signs of movement, but she was very still. He moved his head around as much as he could to try to get a sense of the space around him. He knew nothing about boats, but it seemed to be a fairly small fishing vessel of some kind. There was a small cabin towards the back.

'For God's sake, she's a police officer, Michael. Think about it,' McQueen said groggily. 'They will be scouring the country for her. She'll have left notes. She'll have left a trail that will lead back to you.'

'And they will never know what happened to her, will

The Murder Option

they? It will be a mystery forever. And who knows, maybe because you both disappear at the same time they'll think you ran away together. That would be a kind of romantic twist.'

McQueen's mind was a foggy mess, and the pain from his shoulders, especially the one that had suffered the previous dislocation, was making it even harder to concentrate. But he wasn't ready to give up on trying to talk and reason his way out of this. He just couldn't think of the right words.

'Your sister will crack, Michael,' he said in desperation. 'I spoke to her and she won't be able to carry the guilt. She'll break-down and confess. Stop this now while you can.' But Michael had ceased to listen. He was in his own power-crazed heightened zone now and could only hear his own directions.

'Fifteen more minutes,' he said distractedly. 'Then we will be far enough out where the tides and currents will carry you far, far out to sea. You will never, ever be found. If they were searching with a hundred helicopters and they knew where you were, they couldn't find you. Bit of a storm coming up, too, which makes it even better.' He moved away and went out of McQueen's eyeline as he went into the cabin then McQueen heard the engine slow a little. He tested the bindings around his wrists, pulling at them but without success. They were tight and secure, and cut painfully into his skin when he moved them.

Suddenly, Jarvis was back. 'This is what will happen,' he said, crouching down next to McQueen. 'Anatomically speaking. It's only fair I tell you. First you will go over the side and down into the water and you will sink and drown. That part will be terrifying for you, I'm afraid. Lungs full of water? Trying to breathe while panicking? Oxygen won't be able to get to your brain and you will pass out and then you will die. Then, once you are dead, you will hang there in the water and slowly sink deeper as all the air is flushed from your lungs. Your heart will stop beating, your blood will stop circulating, and very soon the bacteria inside you will take over unchecked. As your body starts to decompose, those microscopic bacteria will produce gases and your body will bloat, which will bring you back up towards the surface, but you will be such a tempting meal that already the fish will have been feeding on you. Nibbling away. The gas will escape, your body fluids will ooze out, and you will sink again, and depending on which fish find you first, you'll be slowly consumed. Eventually it will all be gone, even the marrow in your bones. Your skeleton will remain, way, way down, lying on the bottom, covered in silt for a long time until even that will dissolve. Do you think a fitting end for the great, wonderful, learned Doctor McQueen?'

Jarvis moved away again and then McQueen heard the engine completely stop, and without the forward momentum the boat began to bob even more violently. He turned his head to Tracey whose blank face was near his.

'Sorry, Tracey,' he said, almost sobbing. 'If you can hear me at all, I'm so sorry.'

'What about the rope?' said McQueen when Jarvis was nearer. 'If they do find us by some lucky chance, the rope will show it was murder. I thought you wanted the perfect murder. To be a perfect murder, no one can know.' He was

The Murder Option

hoping Jarvis would slacken his bindings and give him a chance to fight for his life.

'They won't find you,' laughed Jarvis. 'And even if they did find your bones many years from now, I chose this rope because it will rot very quickly in the water. There'll be no sign of it.' He was very proud of himself and he bent close to McQueen's face to grin at him. 'I have thought of everything,' he giggled. 'And I just hope you appreciate how much work I've put in, and the lengths I've gone to just for you, McQueen. I am doing you the biggest favour of your life, making your dream come true, putting your theory into practice.'

McQueen was past trying to ingratiate or appeal to Jarvis's better instincts now. He had none. It was a lost cause, and anger and frustration bubbled from him.

'Don't kid yourself, Jarvis,' he sneered. 'None of this is for me. This is all about you. Your warped mind is somehow trying to justify what you know deep down to be wrong. You were a second-rate student. Did I tell you that? We all laughed when you left. We knew you'd never be a doctor. You were an embarrassment. You failed at every level, and now you think you're good at this because you make up some involved meanings around the murders. But they are nonsense. You're trying to make it into something it's not. But you're just a murderer, pure and simple. And you are stupid, Michael, very stupid. You've made mistakes, and those errors will see you caught.' McQueen was attempting to make him angry, anything that would disrupt the flow, but Jarvis remained passive.

'I outsmarted you, though, didn't I, McQueen? You

should be grateful I've given you these lessons. I've shown you what it means to be truly intelligent, but the class is over now. The bell has rung, and your time is up. Now, stand up.' He shouted sharply and bending over, took hold of McQueen by the shoulders and pulled him into the sitting position, then going behind, grabbed him under his armpits and hauled him to his feet. McQueen's ankles were tied together making it impossible to walk, so Jarvis half dragged, half pushed him to the waist-high side of the boat. McQueen slumped against the side and closed his eyes, if he'd believed in God it was now that he would be calling to him. Reasoning had failed. His dad had been right all along, university claptrap had got him nowhere. He opened his eyes and looked at the peaking waves and the fear in his body felt like a writhing snake squirming inside him with nowhere to go. His thoughts were a scramble and mixed in was a crushing regret. He had never told Julie how sorry he was for the pain he had brought to her life. She'd done nothing wrong, and he'd screwed up the marriage. He thought about Tracey. She would now die at the hands of Jarvis because she had tried to help him, just like the farmer did. He thought again of his grandfather. A man tortured by a past war who had once told his young grandson when badgered for war stories, *"People talk a lot about having rights these days, but the only right you're born with is to a bullet in the head."* It was harsh lesson for a small boy, but it had stayed with him. And then McQueen thought of his dad. Was that to be his final recollection, his dad?

'Thank you,' he screamed into the wind. 'Michael, I want to thank you.'

'What?' yelled Jarvis and spun him round to face him.

'Thank you for my perfect murder,' he whispered quietly, knowing Jarvis wouldn't hear.

'What are you saying?' shouted Jarvis again, his eyes ablaze and leaned in closer to hear what he had said. As he did so, McQueen bobbed his head back and then brought it forward with as much force as he could muster planting his forehead onto the bridge of Michael's nose in a vicious head-butt. He felt the crunch of bone as Jarvis let out a scream and stepped backwards, blinded by pain and blood. At that moment, the boat pitched wickedly, and Jarvis was thrown forward just as Tracey, still lying on the deck, suddenly burst into life. She must have been conscious all along and was simply biding her time, waiting for any opportunity to act. She whipped her tied legs around fast, catching him behind his knees. He stumbled backwards, for a second teetering on the side of the boat, clawing wildly at thin air, his eyes still covered in the blood of his nose. Tracey bucked her prone body and kicked again double footed, catching him in the crotch, and he tumbled over backwards into the water. The sound of the splash and his cries were lost in the noise of the waves. Stunned, McQueen started to shuffle to the place he'd gone in from to see if he could see Jarvis, but Tracey shouted at him from the deck.

'McQueen, get down here. Back-to-back. Untie me before he gets back in. Come on.' It was barked like an order, and McQueen obeyed. He dropped to the deck and wriggled over next to her. Her furious fingers scrabbled at his bindings until, at last, he felt them loosen. Once he had managed to free his hands, he untied her wrists, and then they both untied their own ankles. Standing shakily, they staggered up and went to the side of the boat. There was no sign of Jarvis in the choppy waves. McQueen stared hard at one spot in the water, but Tracey was circling the boat, looking to see if he was anywhere around them. McQueen was torn with a strange mixture of emotion, partly obeying a basic humanity he wanted to rescue a fellow human being if there was even a slight chance. It was what made him different from the murderer who, minutes before, would have happily ended his life, but there was also a big part of him that never wanted to see Michael Jarvis ever again and more than that, wanted him to suffer. It was an ugly thought that he was not proud of and he pushed it away. The vessel was now being thrown around by the waves.

'We've got to get back,' Tracey yelled into the wind which had picked up a lot. 'Before it gets dark. How much do you know about boats?'

'Nothing,' said McQueen.

'Good job I do then,' she answered. She disappeared into the small cabin and McQueen heard the engine turning over. There were some nervous moments as the engine sluggishly coughed and spluttered but didn't start, but eventually he felt a surge of relief on hearing it finally catch. The cabin was no more than a small shelter for the wheel and open at the back. He moved closer and shouted in to her.

'We should look for him. Circle around, maybe.' She shook her head, and he was glad to let her make the cruelly logical decision.

'You can keep an eye out for him, but we have to look out for ourselves right now.' She tapped the gauge next to the wheel. 'There doesn't seem to be much fuel, and the seas are getting really rough. The radio doesn't work. Officially this boat shouldn't even be out here, so we have to hope we can get back. If we do get back we can get them to send out a helicopter to look for him, but I don't give him much chance in this water.'

In the far distance on the horizon there seemed to be a thin outline of land, and Tracey pointed the boat towards it. 'We're in the North Sea,' she said. 'I'm pretty sure that's the east coast, but we can't afford to be stuck out here with no fuel and no radio in a boat this size in any kind of storm.' Even to McQueen's untrained ear the engine was labouring, and he could feel and see that the waves were definitely getting bigger.

'Are we in trouble?' he asked nervously.

'Not yet,' she answered. 'You're lucky. My uncle is a fisherman down in Cornwall. This is how I spent a lot of my summers helping him out.'

'How did you find me at Valerie Baxter's house?'

'Can we do the de-brief later?'

He didn't ask her anything else. He could see she was treating this more seriously than she was letting on. No one respects the dangers of the sea more than someone who has experienced them first-hand, and McQueen didn't want to think about the bitter tragedy of escaping Jarvis only to be lost at sea.

Needing to distract himself, he went to the side and scanned the waves for any sign of Jarvis. For a second, he thought he saw something out there amongst the white froth, something dark. It could have been an arm, but it was only a seal or a sea bird. He flashed a worried glance into the distance. The land didn't seem to be getting any closer. Tracey was hunched over the wheel, one hand nursing the throttle handle, willing the boat onwards through the swell. McQueen could tell by her mood that she wasn't confident about their prospects. There were no life-jackets on-board, another sign Jarvis had not followed any protocols when he'd brought them out to dump them. He hadn't even had one for himself, a mistake that probably cost him his life.

McQueen had no idea how long they had been slapping violently through the waves, but now his eyes were also glued to the horizon. It seemed like an eternity, but eventually their progress had been enough to give a slight release to Tracey's tension, and McQueen saw her nod and smile. They could make out cliffs and could clearly see the land on the horizon. They were at least heading in the right direction, but now Tracey began to worry that without charts or local knowledge they could run aground on hidden rocks as they got closer to shore. They needed help, and taking a captain's role she ordered McQueen to look for any other boats. Finally, they saw another large fishing vessel and altered course, heading for it. After chugging painfully slowly towards the boat, they could see yellow-jacketed men had come to the side to see what they wanted. They pulled close enough to shout and gesture, and make it understood they were in trouble and needed assistance. One of the fishermen disappeared into their cabin and must have made the emergency call to the coast guard because it wasn't long before the white spray of a speeding boat could be seen on the horizon and a coastguard vessel arrived to guide them

The Murder Option

safely back to shore.

As they finally pulled into the small harbour, they could see a police car was on the quay waiting to greet them. Tracey put a reassuring hand on McQueen's forearm and gave it a gentle squeeze. McQueen was unaware he still had the stain of Michael's blood on his forehead, and Tracey chose not to tell him.

'Just tell the truth,' she said. 'Don't embellish or exaggerate. We had to survive against a mass murderer, and we did what we had to.'

It wasn't until McQueen finally stepped off the rocking boat and stood on dry land, his legs shaking beneath him, that the stored emotions of the last couple of days and the overwhelming relief of survival completely washed over him. He felt close to tears. He wobbled and almost fell. He knew how close he had come to death. He had literally stared into the watery grave of his nightmares made real and, for a brief second, even accepted it as his destiny.

After he'd been through heart surgery, several friends had asked McQueen if he'd been scared. The honest answer was no. He hadn't worried for a single second, knowing there were teams of professionals who would be doing their very best to make sure he came out alive. The contrast of facing one determined and focused man who had nothing but killing him on his mind, and had the opportunity to do it, had been terrifying beyond words.

One of the policemen tapped McQueen on the shoulder. He hadn't been aware he had been standing perfectly still, transfixed by the lapping waves in the harbour, but jolted back to the present, he turned now to get into the police car.

Thirty-eight

They sat silently in the back of the police car on a thin blanket. The driver had immediately smelled that McQueen's trousers were reeking and had thrown the cover over the seat, not for comfort but for upholstery protection. They were both taken to a hospital to be given a medical check. In the cubicle, McQueen had been allowed to take off his disgustingly soiled clothes which the nurse put in a bin liner for him to take home, but instead he said they could incinerate them for all he cared. No amount of cleaning was going to remove the traces of terror that had seeped into the fabric, let alone the stench of urine. They'd kindly let him shower and given him some ill-fitting hospital pyjamas to wear instead. The police were keen for him not to be taken home yet as they wanted to get as many answers as possible while the events were still fresh.

The main concern of the doctors seemed to be around the anaesthetic they had been subdued with, but it appeared to have largely worn off by then, although they both still felt a little groggy. The needle marks in his leg and arm were assessed for infection and everything seemed to be fine although blood samples were taken for further tests. The shared needles risk was turning out to be not quite the redundant joke Michael had meant it to be. The doctor who had looked at McQueen said he had been lucky not to have been killed by the drug alone, and that keeping people unconscious while not letting them die was a more difficult thing than people realised.

'He had medical training,' was all McQueen could think to say.

All the usual tests such as blood pressure, pulse, and lungs were showing that McQueen was in pretty good shape for a man who'd been drugged and slung around like a bag of laundry. It only served to highlight to McQueen why mental ill-health went undetected for so long. If there had been a simple bleeping machine that could have assessed his state of mind it might have told a different story.

McQueen was deliberately kept apart from Tracey, and once they had been given the medical all-clear, they were then taken to the police station and questioned separately. She had to be treated as any other witness at this stage as she hadn't been on official police business. They were no doubt looking for any inconsistences in their stories; after all, a man had been lost at sea, but McQueen knew there would be none. His statement took a long time. What started as a few shell-shocked, disjointed mumbled words slowly became a torrent of detail as his story poured out in a cathartic flood. He covered it all, right from the very beginning, right from first being hired by Valerie Baxter, every second he could remember because, for him, it was a release to be able to unburden himself and as there was nothing to hide or lie about, it flowed out easily.

In his account he didn't leave out his feeling he had received no official help from the police in solving the case, in fact he wanted it down on paper that he'd been aggressively warned off the investigation. Coming into the station he'd kept his eyes open for the two uniformed officers who had been to his house but he didn't see them. They were probably keeping a low profile and he didn't blame them. It was an unsolved murder case the authorities had been happy to kick into touch, but through perseverance and insight he had been able to solve. However, Detective Sergeant Brooks, who had originally questioned him over the Bainbridge death, the incident he'd decided was a suicide, was at the back of the room and showed not a flicker of emotion as McQueen detailed the farmer's murder in the murderer's own words.

McQueen managed to avoid the temptation to gloat in his victory and instead gave glowing praise to Tracey. She deserved it, but he knew that in the police press release it would probably be repackaged as all being part of a greater police plan all along.

When he asked about Jarvis, the officer who was questioning him said a helicopter had been sent out to search for Michael in the North Sea, but nothing had been found before dark-fall and that they would try again in the morning, weather permitting. The coast guards weren't very hopeful, however, and it seemed the same fate had befallen Jarvis as he had planned for McQueen, lost without trace, fish food. McQueen remembered the graphic description Jarvis had tortured him with, of how his dead body would decay and be consumed in the water. Perhaps, as it turned out, to be his own death he would have approved, and his own soul would appreciate the closing of the circle.

In giving his version of events, McQueen made sure he mentioned the lecture he'd given on the perfect murder at sea. It was bound to come out sooner or later, and he wanted to be the one to bring it to their attention. He made sure to stress that Jarvis had been trying to enact a lecture topic McQueen had delivered years earlier, and that he and Tracey had been the intended victims.

He'd also asked about Valerie Baxter and what would happen to her, but the officers were reluctant to discuss her other than to say she had been arrested and taken into custody. They did admit, however, she was very distressed and she wasn't making much sense to them so she was undergoing psychiatric assessment.

Eventually, after he'd been over the same details numerous times, McQueen signed his statement and was allowed to go home. Now wearing some borrowed jeans and a t-shirt, he took a cab back to his cold and empty house. When he'd been dragged to the side of the boat, he'd thought he'd never see his home again and closing the damaged door behind him he couldn't quite believe he'd really made it. Once inside, he avoided the comforting whiskey that was calling out to him from the cupboard and made himself a cup of tea instead. The rows of sorted student papers were still laid out on the floor next to the musty boxes. Slumping onto the sofa, his emotions didn't know what to make of it all.

Was he happy to be alive, or traumatised to have been through it? He screwed up his face to stop the tears. Being a psychologist wasn't proving much comfort. He had an academic understanding of what might be going on inside, but the feelings were stronger than he'd expected. He wasn't ready to self-diagnose as suffering from PTSD and wanted to avoid that label if possible. Only the next few weeks would tell how much help he would need. *Physician, heal thyself*, he thought ruefully.

One of the most affecting revelations of the experience had been finding out about Marion Connolly's murder from Michael Jarvis's own mouth. It had been unbearable to be so close and helpless under the power of the man who had taken his lovely Marion's life in a brutal snatch of the essence of her being. It had made him relive the pain of her loss, even though he had been struggling with the fear of his own imminent death. He didn't know how, but strapped to that chair, the realisation of Jarvis's guilt had come to him. It was the clash of the intense emotion, predominantly fear, that had somehow brought the memory to the surface that Michael had been at the college at the right time and he was, in all probability, a psychopath. The pieces had slotted together. McQueen had been looking for any way at all to slow him down, and with a guess he'd managed to unearth the truth. It was still hard to take in, but he knew he would have to tell Marion's family the news before it made it to the press. Anne Kirkpatrick would certainly be hounding him for an interview. Her police sources who had no doubt been keeping her updated had meant he'd already had a text from her.

'Great work, McQueen,' it said. *'You are redeemed. How about an exclusive?'*

He would have to think about that one.

He hoped the Connolly family would see it as closure to find out who had been responsible for Marion's death and to know that her murderer was not going to be able to ever hurt anyone ever again. He allowed himself to exhale in a sigh of muted self-congratulation. His perseverance had made it happen. He'd put an end to Jarvis's reign. That was the other thing about psychopaths, they didn't stop until they were caught.

In his pocket his phone rang, and he scrabbled around to get it out half expecting it to be Anne, but saw it was a call from Tracey instead.

'Hi,' she said. 'You doing okay?' It was comforting to hear her voice. They had shared something beyond words, and he could understand the camaraderie of battle troops a little better now.

'Glad to be alive,' he answered gruffly. 'And a lot better than I might have been.'

'Let's give it a few days until the police have finished their investigations. Then we'll have that de-brief over a glass of champagne. Meanwhile, keep telling the truth. It will all be fine.'

'I owe you,' he managed to get out.

'A few more days,' she repeated, and then hung up.

He went up to bed but, although he was exhausted, he couldn't sleep. His mind kept returning to the catastrophic things that so nearly happened and he had to keep telling himself they *didn't* happen, and that he *didn't* die. McQueen knew from the literature that one of the worst things people do after a trauma or a close call, is to sink into a terrifying spiral of *what if?* It can become a self-torture, and he didn't want that to be the legacy of the event for him.

After many hours, as he started to drift towards the nonsense of pre-sleep, he heard his father's voice growl clearly in his ear. *"I told ya never to ferget the heed, son."*

Of all the books, papers, articles, and journals he'd ever read, the advice that had saved his life had come from his dad. At last he fell asleep, only to find Michael Jarvis was waiting for him, there in his dreams.

Thirty-nine

It was two weeks before McQueen got the call from Tracey to say she felt it was time for them to meet. The police had concluded their investigations and were satisfied with the truth of their stories. She suggested The Fox, a quiet pub with enough room for them to have a private conversation.

There were only a handful of people in the pub that afternoon so they'd had their choice of rugged, beer stained and battered pine tables to choose from. They chose one in a corner away from the bar for their low-key celebration. McQueen had a glass of Champagne sparkling invitingly in front of him but so far it was untouched. Tracey, ever the professional, was sitting with her glass of Diet Coke. They raised their glasses, clinked them together, and then McQueen put his back down.

'How are you now?' she asked. It had been a healing couple of weeks since their joint ordeal, but McQueen was still feeling quite raw.

'Okay,' he allowed. 'I'm still not sleeping great. The doc

said it might be the after-effects of the anaesthetic, but my own feeling is it's down to the trauma.'

'It will fade,' said the policewoman, giving the psychologist some mental health advice. 'Like they say, it doesn't pay to dwell on the past.'

'So,' said McQueen, changing the subject. 'The long-awaited de-brief. I've been thinking about it a lot. How did you come to be at Valerie's house?'

She took a deep breath in readiness to recount her story for the umpteenth time.

'It was down to your friend Tom, really. When you didn't check in with him he got worried about you. First he went to your office and then he went to your flat. He couldn't see you in either place, so he got in touch with me.'

'Did you already know him?'

'No, but he remembered you'd mentioned the name Tracey, and I'm the only Tracey in the station. His worry was that you were lying in a stupor or choked in your room.'

'So good old Tom was the alert,' said McQueen, nodding appreciatively. 'I need to thank him.'

'Yes, you do. I went round to your flat,' continued Tracey, 'and being concerned for your welfare I gained entry to your property, as we say in the force. Sorry about the door, by the way.'

He laughed. It was the most welcome property damage he'd ever had to repair.

'As soon as I went in, I could see you weren't there and I was actually about to leave when I saw the essay you'd put on the kitchen top and the post-it note sticking to it with my name on it.'

The Murder Option

McQueen had been preparing to tell Tracey all about his latest findings and he'd put a note on Michael's essay ready to give it to her once he had verified the alibi, or the lack of it, with Valerie. The note read, *Tracey, this is Michael Jarvis. He wrote about this murder years ago!*

'I read it, and as much of the essay as I needed to. It didn't take long. I saw what you meant. You weren't anywhere to be found so I decided it best to give Valerie Baxter a visit. I knew she was your client, and you'd probably be there. That's when it all started to get weird. As you know, I banged and banged, and I was thinking of forcing entry even though I didn't have a warrant, but then she came down.'

'Thank God you didn't give up and go away,' said McQueen.

'I wasn't going away,' she answered. 'Not until I'd been inside. As soon as she opened the door I knew there was something very wrong. She looked terrified. I asked about you. I told her I was a police officer and she started to come apart at the seams.'

'She was always the weak link in Michael's plan,' McQueen said, nodding.

'That's when I should have called for back-up, but I didn't think my suspicions were enough to go on, and didn't want to have to explain a false call-out, so stupidly I went inside. Bad mistake.'

'Yes, I heard you. I wanted to shout to you, but he put the tape over my mouth.'

'Then chaos,' she said. 'And I handled it so badly. When he came into the kitchen he had his right hand behind his

228

back so I was already wary. As he came in, that's when you started yelling from upstairs. To be honest, I couldn't hear what you were saying, but he was surprised enough to turn to look over his shoulder. As he did that, I saw the needle behind his back, and I pounced and grabbed that arm. He struggled. He was very strong, but I've had some knife attack training and I got his arm in a lock and he dropped the hypo. He was squealing like a baby, crying out to Valerie, and I was telling him he was under arrest, but I'd underestimated Valerie. She circled round behind me and then I felt a ton of wood crash down on my head. I passed out momentarily and when I started to come round it was too late, he was on me with the needle.'

'Jeez,' said McQueen. 'And then the next thing you knew you were on that boat and you had no idea why.'

'All I knew was it wasn't good,' she laughed. 'When I regained consciousness from the anaesthetic, I didn't let on that I was awake, but I was waiting for him to get close to the edge. I knew I'd only get one crack at him. Then when you butted him, I knew it was now or never.'

'My dying regret would have been that I had caused your death,' said McQueen truthfully, a hint of a choke in his throat. 'But instead, you saved mine.' He took a deep breath to make sure his voice wouldn't falter when he spoke again. 'Thank you,' he said trying, but failing, to convey how much he meant it. Tracey shrugged it off.

'We got him, and it hasn't done me any harm at the station,' she said. 'My star is in the ascendency, as they say. We've got a lot of background work to do to make sure this case is as water-tight as possible, if you'll pardon the pun.

There'll be an official inquiry. I was off-duty and investigating a case I'd been ordered to leave alone, which is a no-no, but your voice-activated recorder will be a big help. They've found the boots in his garage, by the way, the Cragtops that match the prints in the field, so it's all good supporting evidence.'

'And what's going to happen to Valerie?' The time spent pleading with Valerie while he was strapped to the chair had not left McQueen with much sympathy for her.

'They are still deciding, but I think there's enough to charge her as an accomplice, unless they decide she was a victim too. That's what her solicitor will argue for sure. Michael had controlled her life ever since they were kids, but the prosecutors will have to gauge how guilty she is.'

'Yes, but victim or not, you can't escape the fact that if she hadn't hit you with that chopping board we wouldn't have ended up on the boat. She did absolutely nothing to stop him taking us out of there in those bags.'

Tracey was nodding. 'I know.' She sipped her coke. 'But no one was more scared of him than she was.'

He knew she was right, but his outlook was still deeply coloured by Valerie's unwillingness to help him when he was at his most desperate.

'Aren't you going to drink that?' she asked, pointing at the Champagne. 'You've earned it.'

'It's just a symbol,' he said. 'I promised myself I would buy Champagne to toast catching Baxter's murderer. You caught him, but I still had to buy it, and now we've made the toast, nothing in the rules says I have to actually drink it.'

'*We* caught him,' she corrected. 'You made all the

connections, you kept at it and worked it out, I only put both big my feet into his crotch.' They both laughed and McQueen could feel some of the burden lifting. *If you can laugh about it, you can deal with it,* he thought.

'So on the back of our devastating teamwork, have you had any more thoughts about joining me in the private investigation game?'

She shook her head and smiled. 'Right now my career is doing just fine, thanks, McQueen. I've got plenty more to do in the police force. There's a lot more I can achieve, so I'll put that one on hold if you don't mind.'

'Okay,' he said. 'I understand. It's still a win for me anyway. At least I have someone on the force I can trust now.'

'You can,' she said, 'as long as you stay on the right side of the law.'

They talked for a little while longer, but both had places they needed to be, and McQueen couldn't find the words to express his gratitude, anyway. There are some things so deeply felt and scary that it's best to leave them alone. McQueen's grandfather had fought in the second world war and had never wanted to talk about any of it. As a child, McQueen had been frustrated he couldn't get exciting war stories out of his grandad and the whole family were never allowed to watch war films on TV. At the time, McQueen as a small boy hadn't understood, but now the grown man felt nothing but sympathy for the pain his grandad had been avoiding. Being trapped on a boat with a killer wasn't the same as years of war, but the distilled fear and sense of fragile mortality had given McQueen a nasty taste of it.

The Murder Option

They left their table, and he followed her out through the pub's gloom to meet the shafts of blinding afternoon light. The full glass of Champagne was still standing, untouched.

SRL Publishing don't just publish books, we also do our best in keeping this world sustainable. In the UK alone, millions of books are destroyed each year, unsold and unread, due to overproduction and bigger profit margins.

Our business model is inherently sustainable by only printing what we sell. While this means our cost price is much higher, it means we have minimum waste and zero returns. We made a public promise in 2020 to never overprint our books for the sake of profit.

We give back to our planet by calculating the number of trees used for our products so we can then replace them. We also calculate our carbon emissions and support projects which reduce C02. These same projects also support the United Nations Sustainable Development Goals.

The way we operate means we knowingly waive our profit margins for the sake of the environment. Every book sold via the SRL website plants at least one tree.

To find out more, please visit
www.srlpublishing.co.uk/responsibility